THE RESIDUAL TOURIST

HAITHAM ALSARRAF

DEDICATION

To all the residual tourists: Tour. Reside. Residualize.

CONTENTS

Picaresque: adjective; noun | ˌpikəˈresk |

Relates to a type of story in which the main character is of a rascal nature who travels from place to place living by his or her wits in a corrupt society. Along the way, he has a series of adventures, often exciting experiences. It is told in first person narration usually without a plot. When pronounced in either British or American English, it comes out as "pick-a-risk."

KUWAIT

When I write, I study the object, moment or experience. I become and live the moment. Words flow out from left to right, indicating the linear process I have to assimilate to so that readers can construe the experience in English. Language being the vehicle. My words being a particular fuel. It is like a dream is written to escape a reality. Or, it is a reality escaping a dream, a filter filtering an already filtered reality. The further the filter, the less clear the reality. The clearer the unclear.

My home office window does not have any curtains. I left it barren. I wanted light to come in and dark to look in. When I write, I want to be somewhere either in the middle. Or, just other. I want to be somewhere afar without the two to define where I am or who I am. Or, what I am.

Across my building is a similar building. There are lots of windows encompassed by heavy concrete. All windows are mirror-tinted during the day. And during the dark, they are welcoming. Light squeezes out around curtains, sifting through protected lives, worrisome living—giving them slight significance, giving them slight meaning. They give them a slight other for a residual tourist.

One of the windows has TV wires outside that are jumbled together coming down from the roof, twisting and turning and leading from one apartment to another to be stuck at a focal point. They all seem to intersect there. In a jumbled mess. There is so much weight. There is so much density in that intersection. All that wiring so people can get their TV shows delivered to them. All those shows so that people can get their filtered truths.

I watch from a filtering building away attempting to unclog their filters, trying to decipher my own.

———

The Khutaaba.

"How much are you willing to pay?" The Khutaaba—the marriage broker—asks about her potential fee. Or, is she asking me about the dowry? She is one of many sprouting female marriage arrangers in the country who are self-described experts in bringing men and women together customarily in an Islamic and traditional culture, which is fast losing its traditions to loose and debauched norms because of a cultural invasion stemming from the West.

Some women come to her because they want to meet someone appropriate according to Islamic principal, without losing the respect of what others may say or think. Others come out of desperation because they have exhausted other methods. From pious women to aging professionals, they would rather marry than be alone.

Aloneness is just unheard of in this part of the world. It is laughed at mostly because it is little understood. Perhaps, even feared.

Being with oneself is a pioneering feat. It may be too

risky for a familial community where religion and family matters define each other. It is just too brave to detach from customs. It is just too dangerous.

People's individual opinions do not matter much. Most are raised in herds to follow protocol. Individual thought like in the West is frowned upon because power comes in numbers, in groups. Anyhow, not much can be achieved if you are not part of one group or another, part of one mafia or another.

And who runs these mafias? More self-proclaimed, power-driven families that have used wealth—not simple riches—to squeeze out other families, influencing politics, finance, and judicial matters in their favor. No wonder we are rated one of the most corrupt countries to do business in. Kuwait is one of the worst for expats to feel happy in, too. And, we hold a top spot for having one of the worst human rights records.

That is in the world.

Definitely in the region.

The Marriage Facilitator—The Khutaaba—is calm waiting for an answer. With each hand, she takes out and places a large Samsung and an iPhone on the table in front, slowly sips on her Turkish coffee, and checks on two different notifications blaring out of the phones before eyeing me again. A plain white hijab veil covers her head. Every few seconds it loosens and she has to fasten. Loosening and tightening. Releasing and adjusting. Rebelling and obeying.

She is also wearing a black abaya over most of her body to cover herself, perhaps to present herself traditionally to earn respect from her possible clients, perhaps to cover much more truth than she is willing to flaunt. The makeup on her face looks like it is a fondue melting off slowly, a transvestite attempt of applying makeup for the night.

She likes to be called Om Ali, which is not her real name but a typical nickname given to mothers in this part of the Arab world. Typical names regardless of which gender may use them wards off suspicion, and it protects against any evil intentions, like how the evil eye is used against malicious attack. Anyhow, such marriage brokers use such popular names because they want to be anonymous, especially in a profession diluted with richly returns.

Om means mother. Ali is a popular Arabic male name. In the Arab and Islamic tradition, it is hoped that fathers and mothers are nicknamed after the eldest son. Continuing a strong patriarchy, even if it is by a woman, helps to broker more marriages. Hence, the famous and widely used Om Ali.

"I'm a natural at putting people together," she says when I ask about why she does this sort of vocation so that I can get a better understanding into why in the hell I am doing this. She sips some more on the medium-roasted, unsweetened coffee, reclines and says, "It's a good human business. It's the kind of business I always saw myself doing." She is retired and this profession brings in much more than her pension gives. The answers I ultimately get are a clear indication that she does not trust so easily, putting me on standby until I ask the right questions. The right way.

Marriage liaisons—khutaabas—gain their reputation by frequenting segregated weddings where they peruse young women. For Om Ali, she probably has sealed many of them into marrying numerous times. Marriage is booming business. Add in special effects like gowns, make-up artistry, catering, and on top of that, the rent of the venue—usually at a five-star hotel—and it is easy to see how marriage in the Arabian Gulf only generates a business mentality instead of an emotional one.

I hesitate, not knowing how to answer The Khutaaba's first question about the type of wife I am looking for.

"What type of woman are you looking for?" interrupting my thoughts. "Are you looking for young or old?" she asks while studying each of my eyes separately.

I am still stuck with the type of woman I may want to marry. I am not fully sure to even why I want to marry.

The air here makes one do things one would otherwise not do in other parts of the world. Every time I land back in Kuwait, I feel negativity. There is definitely something in the air, something pertaining to the land, something connected to an energy gridline. Kuwait is a negative vortex.

"Tall or short?" she continues on. "Slim or matronly? High school or university-educated? Educated in the country or out? Stay at home wife or working?"

She pulls out a large photo album and points at a few faces, flipping the thick pages back and forth, eventually jabbing at some of the pictures on the first page. "This one is beautiful," she tries to guide. "So is that one," moving to the next one. "No, no, she is very beautiful also," and the next.

It is baffling. All this is baffling. It does not feel natural.

Heck, marriage is not natural!

"They cost, though," she tries to sandwich. "They expect their dowries to be in the high end."

"High end?" out of fear I may be paying much more than what I ask for, may be paying for a scam I can not easily get out of. "How high?"

"Thousands over the normal rate," The Khutaaba whispers to herself while sifting through the album, twisting in and out of packed faces that have all been crunched in a folder. All filed in one woman's dossier.

I worry. "Give me a number," indulging her business

know-how. "Like how much?"

Am I buying something or marrying someone?

Her face turns into a Robert De Niro frown, "This one," pointing to the first, "is around 20,000."

Then she looks back because I have not responded as quickly in turn. "If you prefer something a little cheaper, that one," fingering the second photo in line, "is slightly cheaper. 19,000 dinars. It's not that much when you think about how pretty she is, the family she comes from, and she holds an engineering degree."

I pull up my eyebrows in astonishment. Not to the university degree. More to how she is categorizing each person.

After seeing my surprise, she says, "But I'm sure we can negotiate that down a little. Everything is negotiable, habibi."

Habibi? My love? Where—and why—have I heard that so many times before?

The more she speaks, the more I sense it is a business venture. Ordering options, like amenities for a hotel room, is what is. It is a service. Could it be? Could ordering a wife be that unemotional? How in the hell has it worked for so many then? And for so long?

Oh wait. I forgot. Kuwait has one of the highest divorce rates in the world.

If ordering a swift wife through a broker is what many search for, then it would make sense that so many marriages end so swiftly.

There should be experienced and wise people who counsel how to hold on to a marriage, the very mechanics that is takes to hold on and endure a marriage, or any other relationship for that matter. It is the endurance that is a killer. It is harder than having a job in this part of the world. How in the hell does this society expect us to maintain such a lie when the entire foundation is a mess?

Public dating is not allowed, unless you are engaged and chaperoned by an older family member—witness—from the woman's side.

What is left? Why do they not chaperone the marriage as well?

They do not!

Once a couple is married, they move on to the next single person to pressure into marital submission—marital hell.

It is like vengeance for the couples who are already married. I sense they want to make everyone else miserable. Why? Because they have been put in the same scenario. It would not be fair to have someone else be happy in marriage, would it?

It definitely would not be fair either to have someone stay single and actually enjoy it by being detached from this entire mess to begin with.

I meet the first woman I think might be a suitable wife. Her face is pretty, youngish. But I am sure The Khutaaba said she was close to my age. Things can easily get exaggerated in Kuwait.

"Everything is negotiable."

Most discussions actually thrive on exaggerated details. Truth is too dull for most. Lies get people's ears. They seem to add a lot of color to the bland, desert lifestyle.

"I want to be right under Allah," she throws at me. "Are you a true, God-fearing man?" she asks with one of the quietest and most composed voices I have ever heard.

"Well, God is . . ." I try to meander.

She interrupts my thought, "God *must* be important in your life," her voice increasing a tad. "How else can we have a sanctified union if God is not present? God *had better* be present."

Once I hear that, I choose to turn off my words. They are pointless. She clearly fears. The fear does not have to be because of Allah. Just having fear is enough to discontinue talking with her. It would be a waste of both of our time.

"That woman seemed too religious," I point out to The Khutaaba at the next meeting.

"Isn't that what you wanted?" gouging me out with her eyes.

"No! I made it quite clear I was looking for someone secular, a little open-minded, didn't I?"

She looks away, starts opening the photo album and immediately searches for the next candidate. "How about this beautiful creature?" she points and smothers the picture with one of her over-manicured fingers. "I'm sure she'd be a fine spouse."

I pull away the album and flip it around. The woman is attractive. Too attractive, perhaps. I ask, "What sort of family does she come from?"

"A merchant family," speaking through her eyebrows. "An old merchant family. A very solid Kuwaiti family." She waits a little for a response. "I thought the family name wasn't very important to you?"

"It isn't." I just want to know how she describes her clientele—how she exaggerates her products. Trusting women is hard. Trusting Kuwaiti women is even harder. They have been raised to veil themselves in many senses of the word.

Trusting a woman who herds other women and brokers men may be the hardest.

I am not blaming the ones who seek out marriage. They are taught by older women never to reveal too much. Revealing too much of themselves to a local man, or any man, could have adverse effects.

Men have done this to them. Living in a decrepit patriarchy has taught them to be repressed, to be quiet and obedient. To be cunning and wise in their approach to men and marriage.

So why do they want marriage?

The fear of the unknown is perhaps the answer. Being alone is too taboo.

The fear of Islam could be another reason. Islam dictates people's way of life. It composes much of the language, and it directs much of its followers' behavior.

The illusion of freedom is most certainly the reason why many look for marriage. They want to escape their parents' traditions. At least that is what they imagine. Marriage is tough. It should not be approached with ease or negligence.

It takes a whole soul to be in a marriage. It also takes out a whole soul to endure it. But, without any doubt, it takes a whole soul to leave marriage.

The second woman I meet looks materialistic. Jeans and a fancy blouse hold her up to be a woman men should not mess with. Many Kuwaiti women are tough. They may look soft and unthreatening, but they are usually bossy. Her figure is fit. There is little makeup on her face. That is a good sign. Women with little makeup are very likeable.

"What are you goals in life?" she asks right away as if we are on a speed date. "Where do you see yourself in let's say five to ten years from now?" sifting through me like a snazzy accountant. Like a prudent hustler.

She has a typical slightly broken American-Kuwaiti accent, consciously heavily rolling her "r's" and coiling up other consonants like "b's" and "k's." Usually this is a sign that such a woman is over-pampered and bratty, the type that either go to top notch Arabic schools, like the one in the Yarmouk area, or private schools, where the majority of students these days are Kuwaiti.

She tilts her neck and checks on her phone waiting for an answer. Her nose looks like it has been cosmetically altered. It is too pointy, like most women in Lebanon and Iran, who get the same looking nose job.

I do not answer. She obviously wants to be in the lead. To be the man.

"I don't cook, clean or want to take care of kids." She pulls in and pushes out her mobile phone, looking into the screen's reflection as a mirror, lightly fondling the fringes of her hair. "I am not that type of woman, so if that's what you're looking for, then I am *not* that woman," she stresses with that consonant coil. "Please let me know now so we don't waste each other's time. I also expect my husband to provide me a fixed monthly salary, at least one maid, and a driver."

"Don't you work?" I know I asked The Khutaaba to find only women who worked. And I remember her mentioning this one having a master's degree in finance from Boston University.

"I do," she says very calculatingly, "but I still expect the man to take care of most things," telling equally and as mathematically as, "maybe pay for everything."

What use would she be then? Why marry? I need companionship, a partner who will share in the joys and grief of life, not someone who will take advantage of my success for her own betterment.

"Why would any man want to marry you?" I diplomatically ask into her. "What does a woman of your stature have that warrants such excess?"

She carefully puts her phone—her real husband, or temporary boyfriend—down next to one of her thighs. Her head then bends down to her knees with a smile simmering on her face, moving it as a method actor would so often do to get ready to switch roles. She lifts her head back up again and flips her gorgeous, wavy, dark brown hair to the other side and says, "This!" pointing to her face and waving her hands down and back up her body as if demonstrating an immaculate, processed and packaged product. As if it is a timeless piece of art.

"So you think the way you look suffices for a husband to pay for you when you come most likely from a broadminded family who should know better, pushed your own education, have equal rights, and probably a very strong-paying job?"

"Yes!"

No thanks!

No wonder there are so many divorces!

It would be cheaper to find a non-Muslim foreigner instead. I would not need to pay a dowry. She would likely care more humanly rather than view me as a commodity, and the marriage will surely last much longer.

Maybe I just need to find myself first. Maybe, I just need to drown myself first.

No wonder so many Kuwaiti men marry foreigners. It is absurd and highway robbery to marry a woman from a developing country who demands more than a woman from a developed nation.

No way!

I can not understand it. I am not some young man looking to marry a younger woman. Demanding a lot would then make more sense. I am middle-aged, divorced, and already have children.

I thought women around my age are less fussy compared to ladies in their twenties. Kuwait has so many single and divorced women in my age group. Why are they still fussy? They should be grateful for anything half decent coming their way.

I used to be like them, but that was when I was younger, in my 20's. Something in my gut is telling me that thinking of any relationship right now would be a massive mistake.

Why am I thinking of marriage? I just got out of one.

Loneliness. I want to be validated for all that I have made myself into. I do not want to feel like I am fading while I am living. Is my worth only seen in what I produce, in how I help to monetize other people's pleasures?

No wonder when we have Mother's Day in this part of the world, there is little to no mention or care given to men, to fathers who have given so much but who have been neglected. Is it because, as a husband and father, I dared to care so much, because I dared and risked my own inner spirit to provide for my wife and children so they could have a comfortable life, a life much more worthy than anything I received as a son growing up? Is it because I worked hard in an office and tried to earn so much that I was seen to have neglected my home life?

Well, no one taught me how to feel when I was growing up. I was raised as a machine, as a man, to be a perfect soldier. I was raised not to cry, not to show emotion, not to complain. I was raised to be an ATM machine. Raised to cater to a future wife and kids, catering to anyone else but myself.

All I have asked in turn was to be validated. All I have wanted was to be justified for simply being a man who has tried his best to love others but is one who is full of holes, full of derangements. Full of decay.

Mother's Day does not even officially exist in this part of the world. That term has been inappropriately dubbed, showing favoritism towards just one parent. The day we have is formally called Family Day, when every member in a family should be celebrated.

Companionship is not worth it if I am forced to be desperate. And I am expected to pay for it through a marriage broker and a wife, as well as surrender my own convictions for a woman's.

And many women here believe they do not have equal rights!

I would rather take my chances being alone.

———

Driving to Kuwait City, the traffic is backed up. This is the norm. Expect to be delayed hours for some place that is very few kilometers away. I normally talk to myself. It is because I drive alone. Live alone. A voice in my head starts talking in a Beiruti, Lebanese accent, elongating certain vowels, dancing my eyebrows up and down quickly to accentuate and dramatize the words. Maybe there is a tinge of Syrian in there, too.

"Shoo, moo ajbaack, habeebee?" come out as, "What, it doesn't impress you, darling?"

"La, moo ajaabnee, habeebtee," is the response meaning, "No, it doesn't impress me, female darling."

The rest of the dialogue is a wrestling match between the Lebanese male with the female.

Perhaps there is a little Syrian in there, too.

The actual content is unimportant. Back and forth, they throw eventual slurs and insults to destroy, to show their affection for each other.

This is how I amuse much of my driving time.

When I am stuck.

On the Feheheel Expressway, I see a bus and a Chevrolet Tahoe both parked on the slow lane, jamming other cars behind, resulting in heavy, variously loud honking sounds. One man in a baseball cap and a long garmented dishdasha is huffing and puffing, holding a wooden stick trying to open the bus driver's door. The door is locked. The man continues to nervously huff and puff.

It is still a highway.

Can people be that moronic?

Cars are zooming in between and around both trying to get to somewhere, usually the place is unimportant. Drivers just seem to have to get there, before you and anyone else, no matter if they injure or kill themselves along the way.

Why is everything rush, rush, rush; where are they going? Only one tenth of the tiny country is developed, and it is developed vertically.

Cars can't drive up buildings? Or, can they?

Temperatures are pleasant today, so heat can not be blamed for their hurry, like it is often done most of the year. Blaming one thing or another is part of the Arab hypochondriac nature.

Anxiousness is the norm.

I turn on the radio to listen to classical music as I pass the fight that I will read in one of two local English newspapers. Both news outlets usually sensationalize local stories about crime and illicit and immorally un-Islamic acts. Articles about prostitution and drug busts are communicated mythically, in tall tale description. Usually, the gay and transgender community is blamed for acts that many supposed heterosexuals exercise. Then, out of Kuwait, on social media websites, truer versions expose how the police brutally and sexually violate the same people they catch, hiding much more of the never-ending bisexual nature that many practice here, whether by authorities, or other.

Other.

And, jumbled wires.

Most of the other international stories are quoted directly from their sources or poorly paraphrased and summarized. Why does this happen? Management is key. Look at how hierarchies are designed here then it will be easy to understand how corruption works. How it massages its way into every fabric of this society.

Everyone has one form or another of clout and connections called wasta. If everyone has it, then does it not cancel itself out? It is simply corruption then.

Just call it corruption.

A bus with South Asian workers zooms by me on the emergency lane. The fast lane. People are fed up with the systemic double-dealing, sleaze and criminality increasing in the country. But money keeps most coming, keeps most staying here. Keeps most dying here.

They are in the country to exploit and reap the benefits of the strongest currency in the world. Much of it will be remitted, though. Then the Central Bank would allocate and tighten money supply to keep the Kuwaiti dinar's worth stable. Exporting oil is failing to be enough for a growing population, and for a more fraudulent populace.

I move to the slow lane just in case the herd, who thinks the fast lane will get them quicker to wherever they are going, congests it. I start up another dialogue between myself and I. The setting is at one of the over-employed government ministries.

"Yeah friend, what kind of corruption can I help you with today?" I say with an unnecessarily thick voice.

"I need a favor. Could you process my papers without waiting weeks? Every document is fully filled out and numbered."

"Sure dear friend, one corrupt process for a corrupt

friend coming corruptly right up!"

That is how people should speak to one another. They would rather use charades and plastic behavior to insinuate than be blunt and candid.

I guess honesty is just not pretty enough, not distanced enough. I guess sincerity is just too close, too ugly.

Anyhow, I stop talking to and with myself.

"To" indicates one direction. "With" indicates together.

I switch stations to a local radio program. A woman expert is talking about driving behavior. She recommends that drivers keep their cool when other drivers behave rudely, because if we rage against someone cutting off or driving speedily past us on the emergency lanes, it will manifest into spiraling stress for ourselves, which will not help our stability the rest of the day, or week. Or, lifetime.

The expert is another foreigner, who probably has not lived here long enough to fully comprehend our unique driving habits.

We all lose ourselves; we all lose control. We should all lose control of ourselves to know who we are. To know how much other people's control actually dials us.

Losing control helps to understand how to manage self-restraint.

We are only human, after all.

"The trick is to withhold," she says. "It may have been arbitrary. Even if it wasn't, try to think in the other driver's shoes. It may help you to control your surroundings, controlling any aggravated stress in your immediate environment."

That sounds all swell and dandy if it were in a country where drivers have more regulation and respect for one another, where such incidents happen once in a while. Here, however, driving in the middle of two lanes, cutting off every few seconds, infectious tailgating, and randomly flashing head lights to remove drivers out of the way is a minute to minute occurrence.

The expert is a woman. The host is a woman.

I am not.

What about the men whose biological makeup is different than women's? Violence is part of our nature. That does not mean we need to use physical violence. Swearing off the other driver's mother or insulting the country he comes from—in his dialect and accent—seems to calm me. No fights have to ensue.

Why is that not talked about as therapy, as self-control?

She should discuss how to learn courtesy for the drivers who start this mess to begin with. Cap the problem before it arises. Then stress would not have to be manifested and spread.

Bandaging a broken infrastructure is not the answer!

Driving slowly with lots of space behind a large half lorry, a sea of red break lights come alive once I go over a bridge. An accident has caused more traffic.

Spectating is popular here.

A brand new Ferrari apparently drove under a Volvo sedan, pushing the Volvo up from behind, making it virtually stand straight up on its front end. A woman driver is standing to the side of the Volvo goggling her smart phone. A young male punk is standing next to the Italian luxury, shouting at a young policeman.

Another policeman is waving drivers to continue moving. No one is obeying him. They are more interested in the spectacle of the accident. It seems to give them cause, give them purpose, some sort of amusement, to certainly gossip about to their friends, which is Kuwait's version of social media. It has been tested, time and time again. It has been perfected.

I honk at the half lorry, as these sorts of skinny

Japanese trucks are called. I believe the Brits ingrained the phrase on us when Kuwait was a protectorate of theirs.

Yeah, protectorate, not colony like the United Arab Emirates or Bahrain.

Instead of speeding past the accident, the half sorry of a lorry brakes instead, knowing all too well that its rear steel bumper would smash up my weak—illusive—front American bumper if I were to ram him. Then I would get blamed for the accident, because according to local traffic laws, I would have to pay the vehicle I hit in front, no matter whose fault it is.

But what is trickier according to local laws is if a non-Kuwaiti has a physical fight with a citizen, then he would immediately be deported, regardless of whoever starts it.

The traffic police seem to be trying, but their numbers do not compare to the overwhelming numbers of vehicles that herd tightly and break off from the crowd when they want to break rules to get to their destinations.

Breaking off from wires.

Usually, their destinations are near.

The government and a select few families who run this tiny state have lost control of their own creation; allowing in two thirds of noncitizens in ratio to citizens will surely bottleneck the streets, if not the country's progress. How are people supposed to get to school and work on time if poor planning causes them to be late? Do the powers that be not care about their own investments?

And what about the Kuwaiti drivers themselves? They think they are invincible and untouchable when it comes to laws. One should look at oneself before blaming others.

Yeah, do not worry. I blame myself plenty.

Thank the weak government for the mess. If one chooses to be in authority, then demonstrate it authoritatively.

My destination is Souq Sharq in Kuwait City, or East Market, as it is translated. The place used to mostly be waterfront for old dhow fishing boats until a certain family sought it out as a potential site for commerce. They got the go ahead from the country's rulers to build it into land and a marina, but then have had to turn around and rent it from the same rulers.

Today is February 25th. Kuwait celebrates National Day as an independent country, as a young nation. People are getting ready to drive on the Gulf Road to honk, cheer, and spray foam and water at each other.

I guess such antics commemorate the country's independence.

Some wires need to stay tangled. Perhaps buried.

The famous colors of the Kuwaiti flag will drown out anything else. The ruling family has been using multiple channels to spread nationalism. Money is not a big issue. That is because much of it is thieved by way of all the oil that is sold to the world. If Kuwait produces around 4 million barrels of oil a day, and if the yearly average rate is $55 a barrel, then $220 million a day is the result before other costs like salaries, refining and shipping. That is over $80 billion a year for a 1.4 million population of citizens.

Come on!

The government does not even pay the monthly salaries. They have handed that power to an autonomous and diplomatic body that handles all the monthly public salaries. The country's sovereign fund does it all, and most Kuwaitis do not even know it. Kuwait Investment Authority (KIA) is the fourth largest national fund in the world that handles over $550 billion of the country's investments, most of it internationally. The same families that run the country, and created a driving and socially corrupt mess, are the ones that get the jobs at KIA.

The ruling family is trying desperately to cover why Kuwait was invaded, occupied, and annexed in 1990 by its northern neighbor—Iraq. They even paid every citizen 1000 KD on the same holiday a few years ago during the Arab Spring uprisings. They think that by swamping people, especially the youth, into believing that Kuwait is a country worth fighting for—or paying off—that much of what happened during that war will be forgotten. Or misinterpreted to cover the real shame they did in order for Iraq to invade this tiny but rich nation.

At the top portion of the flag, moving from left to right, is green. It represents "our lands." The color underneath is white, which signifies "our deeds." The last horizontal color is red. It is supposed to stand for "our swords." The one color that holds all three colors together is a black trapezoid—a wire—meaning "our battles."

There are already families setting out lawn chairs on the few grass parcels Kuwait has. Such grass is not native to the arid desert. It requires a lot of water to maintain. Most of it comes from the desalinization plants, where reverse osmosis is used to filter out salt to create brackish water, mostly advised for horticulture.

Bottled water, whether imported or assembled in the country, is more expensive than 91-octane gasoline. 91-octane is the lowest grade in Kuwait. So, water is an expensive resource that people should take care of.

Anyhow, families bring their chairs, picnic blankets, large amounts of food and large families to sit on the very scarce grass. Many will litter and not pick up after themselves. No oversight, accountability and enforcement lead to such behavior.

It sounds familiar, does it not? Oh yeah, the local government and handful of families that control this emirate.

Cars are deliberately driving slowly, honking, celebrating Kuwait's independence. They have Kuwaiti flags hanging out of their windows as well as stickers that sheath back windshields, hoods and trunks. There is much pride in Kuwait's history. Most of the faces are smiling, but they are young smiley faces for a kidnapped history. They probably have no idea what people truly went through in 1990-1991 to get Kuwait's independence back from Iraq's Saddam.

I was caught up in that seven-month occupation as a young man. No one taught me who the real enemy was. Was it my own corrupt and often lazy citizens, or was the enemy the Iraqi soldiers who too did not know why they were sent to invade a neighboring Muslim ally? Things blurred then. This mess now is the result.

Most of Kuwait's population is youth and adolescence. They were born during or immediately after Kuwait's February 26, 1991 liberation.

Two young boys are standing on a curb, waiting to spray passersby with water. Their clothes and faces are painted in the Kuwaiti flag.

No one is supervising them.

Waving flags and painting faces with the same flag is too nationalistic. Too many greens, whites, reds, and blacks all over the streets today create a false love. Nationalism had been a strong weapon in the past, when citizens believed and respected their government. Since the war, much of it has diminished.

The evidence is in how a large number of Kuwaitis leave the country during the 25th and 26th. They would rather be tourists than patriots. They would rather be temporary expats than nationalistic citizens. The evidence is also in how ordinary citizens use wasta among themselves to get by without the government's help. Why?

Because the government has used favoritism to corrupt the country so much that citizens have fought back by trying to stymie the corruption by using their own nepotism, creating a bigger criminality that has become the normal behavior.

What is seen as help between the corrupt here is actually a degenerative disease quickly transcending into a civil war.

Across the street is a traffic police car. Two young policemen are standing outside the passenger side. One of them is talking into the microphone part of his white earphone. The other is scrolling his phone.

No one is supervising them.

On the intersection between the boys and policemen is a long and thorough bed of colorful flowers wrapped by red bricks. Turf grass complements the flowers and bricks. All of it looks like it is from another country, a country with a hospitable climate. All of it looks too much like a mirage, covering the natural pale desert with colors foreign to the region.

Covering wires with the most expensive currency.

There is a street cleaner in a yellow uniform tugging a large plastic waste container. He is not malnourished. In fact, his stomach looks bloated. Actually, too bloated. That is usually a strong indication that he is eating plenty of rice compared to a thin stomach seen back in his Indian subcontinent.

No one is supervising him.

Every few feet, he stops to sweep dust and light garbage off the turf grass. A woman suddenly stops her car in the fast lane. She gets many honks behind her. She pulls down her window to hand the street cleaner a donation. The cleaner bows a few times and puts back his face of sorrow and again stops every so often to sweep, until the next victim surfaces.

Usually a woman.

Scores of dhows are coming in to dock. Seagulls are swarming above them. Fresh catches are about to be unloaded for sale. Cats are pulling in from different corners. So are many fish aficionados.

As I continue to scope the bay, I catch a woman sitting alone on a bench nearby looking at the same thing. She is wearing the all black abaya and niqab, traditional clothing to ward off prying eyes. Even her hands are covered in black gloves. The only skin showing is her eyes, and they are tightly tucked and veiled behind the niqab.

What is it like to be a woman living behind a costume, to be a woman who sees much of the world instead of baring naked for the world to see? Women who wear this type of clothing are often ridiculed in Europe and the United States because they are viewed to be repressed and oppressed by men, by a man's religion.

She suddenly pulls up the bottom portion of her face veil and inserts a bottle of water to drink from. Trying not to look conspicuous, I look towards the boats, but I am secretly staring at her. I can see her pearl white skin. Her cheeks are a little rouged like her lips. It must be very hot and itchy having unnatural materials covering natural skin for long periods of time. Her eyes pull toward my direction just a little. She knows I am examining her, but it does not seem to deter her from hydrating herself.

She removes the bottle and carefully allows the veil to fall back down. Her composure is statuesque; barely any movement happens. I am sure she is used to having people stare at her. She most likely stares at many more people. Her clothing hides so much, but it also allows so much for her to uncover by looking out into the world. It is like a structure or container that is positioned on a sidewalk or road. People pass it, yet they rarely think about how it watches them.

I continue to study, watching her body, her behavior, her secret world. The edges of her eyes are hydrated with kohl. The black powder beautifies yet shields her, producing captivating all-seeing eyes. She is blocked off from this insane world. Peaceful in the way she examines the world without being probed and examined in the same manner in return. She is watching everyone. No eyes are unveiling and stripping her.

It is beautiful. She is beautiful, even though I can not see her natural skin. The skin she wears on the outside makes any love that comes her way worth the sacrifice and pain to get hers. She wears so many layers to ward off unnecessary worldly pains, hiding an undisclosed world within, protecting it from evil, shielding herself from her own ugliness of a human race. The way she remains still is like a subterranean world, like a middle earth. Like an earthly paradise hidden in public sight.

She is a void on to herself, a chasm waiting to be discovered.

The Conspiracy Theorist is supposed to meet me at the fish market portion of Souq Sharq. He is a Kuwaiti bachelor who has been excommunicated from his family's wealthy inheritance. As a Christian minority, and what many of his family and friends may see as a conspiracy nut job, he is living in an undefined, conceptual area. He has a streaming income from a job he does not go to. One of his family's private companies employs mostly non-Kuwaitis. The high management at the company, who are all foreigners, have asked The Nutter not to come, but they pay him a full monthly salary. They regard him too inefficient and too wacky to work, but since the company belongs to his family, they pay him off to shut him up.

Things work in reverse in Kuwait.

So, he lives in an unclear buffer zone between traditional, Islamic practices and the religion of commerce. And he strives to bring light to his Christian faith, but more of his and spiritually esoteric faith, in the middle of the two.

We are to meet where the dhows dock and disembark because he says he has something to show me. While I wait, I see Asian fishermen unloading fresh heaps of zubaidi, hamour, and shrimp to be sold for morning sale. Hamour is a grouper sea bass, which is one of my favorite Kuwaiti dishes, especially with well prepared basmati rice and mixed spices.

Basmati rice, chai and biryani are major staples of the many dishes that are not indigenous to Kuwait. An arid climate does not allow for such growth. Dhows brought them back here from India during the seafaring days.

Past all the boats and seafood, I look out and into the water's expanse. The waves are calm, but the water is not the typical bluish green. Today, it looks silvery. Currents are gently ebbing and flowing. They are dancing in a pleasant, localized delirium.

"Hey, brother," I hear coming behind.

The Conspiracy Theorist and I greet with handshakes, no customary cheek-to-cheek kissing. The first thing he does to interrupt our flow is take out a cancerous cigarette. His eyes squint because some of the smoke starts migrating up his face, through his eyes.

His is screening. That is what he is doing.

His eyes are screening the smoke, screening the haze, probably about to screen me like he does everyone else.

"Look behind you," he says. "You see that forty-story erection?" asking about the towering building across the street. "That's the new Central Bank."

The new Central Bank of Kuwait is pyramid in shape with a truncated tower. At the very top is an all-glass viewing platform, which is not open to the public, he tells me. When it is lit, it lights up from the inside as well as the outside, shining like a lighthouse. Shining like a beacon probably closely associated with Freemason symbology.

"Is that an all-seeing eye?"

"Yep." He strokes back his lengthy bald head a few times. "It'll be visible out across the Arabian Gulf."

"Really?" eyeing the pyramidal obelisk shaped pillar. It looks like a capital A, but the top part shaved off.

"Why would such a towering structure be needed in Kuwait when the previous one located a few hundred meters away was running smoothly?" he asks, asking himself more it seems.

It is located near the Grand Mosque and Seif Palace, where the Emir of Kuwait resides.

"Why build the bank next to an Islamic place of worship?" continuing to probe, smoking in a heavy huff. "What is The Family trying to tell us?" asking with his eyes. "That Egyptian symbolism and Islam are closely connected?"

I push him. "Go ahead. Tell me!"

Instead, he goes into a further round of self-questioning. "Could it be that the bank has been run over by a local Illuminati family dictating financial policy to the main cabal in Europe and its desire to spread east, into Iran, Central Asia, and eventually into China?"

"Local Illuminati family?" I stress because I am a little confused.

He says, "Ohh yeahh!" ever so calmly. "They are everywhere," staring at a parking lot behind us and then across the street at the century-old mud buildings. "Look at where the building is facing," looking out to the water.

"The building faces Iran," he throws out with his chin.

Why would this bank be standing tall directly facing Iran? This is what I ask myself. Just a few years ago, the expanse of water dividing Iran in the east and the Arabian countries in the west was generally called the Persian Gulf, the very same name addressed by the Brits when they gorgeously demarcated Arabia and appointed their own Arabian puppets to rule until the present time. Now, the Americans are allied with the Brits in the Gulf, but the regional Arabs want to transform history by rewriting and perhaps expanding their lost drive for conquest. The Arabian Gulf is a very recent term pushed by these governments to wield a greater influence, starting off from this region.

Iran remains silent. Watching. Waiting.

"The Rothschilds!" The Conspiracy Theorist says. "Did you know that they and every single monarchy in Europe marry each other only because of one reason?"

"Wealth?"

"Blood type!" he exclaims with confidence. Every single one of them, one hundred percent of them, every single one of them is a negative blood type," he says calmly as if it is widely known. "Dude, they are the chosen people. They are the meek who have inherited the earth."

"Come on, really?"

"Brother, they have created all the wars, famine, economic depressions, mass media brainwashing, and they are about to sweep through Iran all the way to China and Russia. The Muslim world does not have negatives. They are very rare."

"I'm negative."

"Really?" his face less animated. "You are one of the lucky ones then."

"Are the Hezbollahs positive bloods then?"

"Negatives."

"All of them? Even the ones in southern Lebanon and Iraq?"

"No, the ones at the top in Iran are. Them only as far as I know."

"That doesn't make much sense. Why would the Illuminati want to kill off their own types?" I ask.

"They won't. They'll kill off many in between, many who serve under. Ones in power will not die off. They are ordained to serve."

Ordained? Is The Nutter that much of a nut job? Or, is he that wise? Only wise men who dig this deeply and correlate theories with known facts are actually awakened. No wonder his family, friends, and employers have disowned him. He is a danger. Too dangerously bright.

"Did you know that every president in the US has been negative? The only one who wasn't was Martin Van Buren, the eighth president who served from 1837-1841. That guy was the first president born on US soil. He was the only one who wasn't a British subject."

Okay, I think I am getting an overload.

I ask him how he thinks Van Buren was allowed to preside over the nation if he was not part of the other members of the mafia. He postulates that he was allowed to win because the negatives back in Britain wanted havoc to ensue in the young US. Soon after Van Buren was in office, the country went into economic shit.

"Forty-four out of forty-five have been negative blood types," slightly angrily. He says, "Believe that shit?"

He examines the very top portion of the Central Bank. "Most successful people, most celebrities, most influencers are negatives, brother. Angelina Jolie, Brad Pitt, Tom Hanks, Johnny Depp and so many, many more are negatives, bro. That's why they've reached the top so quickly. Talent is not why they are famous. That's why they are untouchables. The paparazzi are not allowed to hound them. In fact, they are told to move away from them. Or else!

"Am I the only one who is seeing this, or am I that crazy? The culling is coming," he says like Brando's "The horror. The horror" in *Apocalypse Now* while stroking his head. He slows his tempo and utters, "It's coming. It's coming."

"How in the hell do you know all this?"

"I just do," he says. "I'm a negative!"

I add in describing what I know about the region, "Opium is flourishing in the Middle East. Since the US invaded and warped Afghanistan early in the 2000's, they took over most of the poppy fields, burning a few time to time to fool most of the world into thinking they are stomping out the drug trade. Most of it is funneled through Iran, Iraq and Central Asian countries like Kazakhstan and Turkmenistan upward into Russia. The outcome? Heroin use has been on a dramatic rise in these countries. And Kuwait is no exception."

He returns with, "There are now so many addicts in Kuwait that it is tearing up the society. And who is helping the spread and sale locally?"

"Who else? The ruling family," I say.

"Yes, brother, The Family."

Kuwaitis call the family in power ruling, not royal. Tourists and expats call them royal. They were, and still are, a Bedouin tribe that acted as mediators between other Bedouin tribes. They have been elected. They have been selected. Not the type of elected seen in Western democracies. No. They were put in, but they have corrupted their power, which has created a social and economic vacuum amongst everyone else in the country.

They are not supposed to entangle themselves in business and perhaps other parts of society. However, different parts of the prominent side have now come full circle by controlling and monopolizing practically every point of that circle, principally since protests led by other Bedouin families started a few years back.

"The white side of the ruling family is negative," The Christian Theorist says. "The dark side is positive, as far as I know."

"How do you know?" I ask.

"I just do," he says a little aggressively. "The dark side will never, and I mean never, be allowed to rule. The slaves won't rule," he emphasizes.

"But they did, didn't they?"

"If you are talking about right before the current Emir, then yes, but that short span before his sickly death was allowed to happen. To shut up the darker side so that they were given a chance to rule as promised."

Why must so much be placed on creating mirages here, I ask myself? Why so many smokescreens?

Strolling past the dhows and closer to Seif Palace, he points out to the Gulf, towards Bubyan Island. One of the largest seaports in the Gulf is being built on Bubyan. It is a large island to the northeast of Kuwait City, near where the Tigris and Euphrates Rivers meet and flow out into the Arabian Gulf.

The Persian Gulf.

The Theorist states that the Rothschilds and their local Illuminati families want Kuwait to build the largest seaport in the area and strangle Basra slightly to the north, keeping Iraq dependent on their security and economic aid for a long time while hijacking their oil. Just like they have done in Tunisia, Libya, Egypt, and sweeping east to the Gulf countries. Syria is in the works, but it is proving to be a challenge.

I start putting pieces together and surmise that is why all those overhead bridges going in and out of Kuwait City to the north, and the current seaport in Shuwaikh, are being developed.

"There you go, negative blooded brother!" he says. "Once people connect the dots, theories then become facts. The government is trying to recreate the Silk Route. The whole Bubyan fiasco is about Silk City," he states, pivoting his feet back and forth while remaining still. "They want to create a city that will house over 700,000 people. Masonry will be everywhere, from the designs of the city to the purposes. In the highest building in the center, there will be a United Nations department that will come with the same Luciferian religion that the Illuminati practices, including a synagogue."

Now, why would a Lucifer-based temple be allowed? Why would a synagogue be allowed here when Kuwait removed all known Jews a century ago and publicly kept its distance from Israel ever since? What does all this have to do with the Silk Road?

"The Silk Route will connect Kuwait by water and land to and throughout Central Asia," theorizing away. "That is why the Gulf countries are building a linking train system."

The Conspiracy theorist stops pivoting. He turns off his phone, stashes it in his back pocket, takes a deep breath, and says, "Nothing will happen here," with a stiff, indifferent look. His face is too serious. I have rarely seen him like this.

Then he says, "There won't be any war in the Gulf countries because this is planned with the West, with the Illuminati, to expand east. Most of the Emirs in the Gulf are crypto Jews, but they pose as Muslims, as the protectors of Islam in the region, in clearly Saudi Arabia. That's why

Israel never intimidates or bombs us because our rulers are Jews who further their agenda to create an Israeli megastate that stretches from Israel to parts of Syria, Iraq, northern Saudi Arabia, and most of Kuwait. From the Mediterranean to the northern Arabian Gulf."

I ask him, "Is that why Qatar is now the richest country in the world per capita?"

"Why do you think Qatar never has any terrorist problems in their country?" he asks, emphasizing "terrorist" in a southern American accent, poking fun at how southerners are easily swindled into believing what they are told on their news channels.

"The Qataris have American think tanks like the Rand Corporation there, with their Central Command in Doha. They and their Jew partners have created ISIS, the fake fundamentalist Islamic organization to overthrow entities that challenge their doctrines. We all know what a joke ISIS is, but in the US, they think it's real. That's because the few media outlets that control the world are completely run by the Rothschilds. They own up to ninety something percent of the world's wealth. If you can't see it, you will never understand what I see."

"Believe me, I understand," I say with a squirmed face.

"Have you heard of the Jewish tribe of Dan?"

"I have. Why?"

"I think I am from the lost tribe of Dan. They were negatives. They scattered west across the Mediterranean and up into Europe. Then they created their monarchies. Brother, I think you might be one too."

"That'd make more sense than what I was born into. But there's a difference between Pharisees and Hebrews. Most people mistake Hebrews as only Jews. Pharisees, strangely, sounds like Farsi, doesn't it?"

"Damn, it does!" The Theorist excites.

"They were tied up all along this Gulf and Arabia. Iran has the most Jews after Israel in the Middle East. Morocco close behind. Iraq has one of the densest concentration of negative blooded Jews in the world. It makes sense that they kidnapped the Hebrew way of life and used it to control others as the first Abrahamic religion."

"Ah. Maybe it had nothing to do with religion. Maybe it had to do to with our rhesus negative blood type."

"Wow! Either way, Arabs are Semites and Jews are Semites. It's funny whenever a Jew yells out 'anti-semite' to an Arab. What a joke!"

He goes further and describes how the pineal gland is an essential energy point located in the lower middle forehead. When it is not opened, usually because of fluorided water and calcium build up, the human mind is contained. It is controlled by the Illuminati to serve them in an illusory world called reality so that the negative bloods continue to exercise power while holding on to their extraterrestrial secrets.

"Negatives are aliens?"

"Oh yeah! Our DNA has been tampered with."

I take a few minutes to digest the alien connection, but it makes sense. It makes sense in how I have always been odd in a world full of conformity. "Yeah, but not all negatives are bad people, are they?"

"No, just the walk-ins," he says. "They are the Rothschilds and a few others who actually came from the Anunnaki's Sumerian city, which is a three hour drive north of us."

"Basra?"

"Yes."

The Haras.

"It's government regulation," The Haras says as I hit the elevator button to go up to my little matchbox apartment, a little new luxury of a civilized jail cell. The handles do not fully latch, the air-conditioner blows out more sound than air, and the whitewashed walls already have long and deep cracks running down them. These are how new apartments are constructed in Kuwait. The Haras—the building guard—shouts the same words at the end of each month when he expects his 10 dinars, half for the trash service, the same service he takes down to a bigger container out on the street. The other 5 is for washing the car. "It's government regulation."

Camelshit! There is no such law, but he sure knows how to hustle like most Egyptians here.

"Where's the damn toilet seat?" I lay into him about a Chinese-made plastic crap that broke instantly once I sat on it. "I asked for it months back."

"Wallahi," he starts recoiling, "I asked management . . ." camelshitting his way out, and flipping it around, "Where were you in Ramadan? Tenants who asked for them got them."

"Out of the country. You already knew that. I told you."

"It's only 2 KD."

Wallah is an Arabic expression meaning I promise by God, strengthening any credibility on other expressions that normally come after. Egyptians and others around the Levant may use an "i" sound at the end to indicate the Kasra vowel, which sounds like a short "e." Vowels are not part of Arabic letters. Vowels instead accentuate them above or below. People from the Gulf simply use wallah.

"Wallahi, how come that TV wire dangling outside my bedroom window hasn't been removed by the family under me? Those kids are loud, too. How is a large family allowed to live in a tiny apartment anyhow?" drenching him as he often tries to do when I am coming home exhausted to death.

"Wallahi . . ." he begins.

I interrupt him, "Wallahi, the wire is illegal."

He laughs at his own medicine.

Before he tries to utter another syllable, I tell him: "Wallahi, it's government regulation."

Wallah is considered a Muslim sin when misused, especially if it is followed up with a lie. Yet, it is widely thrown like inshallah, which means God-willing.

Rains have flooded many parts of south Kuwait lately, far passing the yearly average. The government has given holidays to all ministries, schools, and told everyone to stay home because they do not know how to adequately handle such a mess. Improper infrastructure, like street drainage, has wreaked chaos.

Even private entities like the stock market decided to close. Most of the transactions are done online. Why close it? That does not bode well when it just got accepted as an emerging market.

The army has been called in, too. Ministers fired, blame thrown around by puppet parliament members—the 9th cabinet since 2006—because of corruption and shitloads of "wallahis."

For those working in the public sector, it has some advantages. Salaries are paid per month, not per hour, regardless if one comes in or not. Regardless if the government gives holidays to tame weather they have not planned well for because of dishonesty in its ranks. And, since tomorrow is Thursday, no one will go in to work. The excuse will be: "Wallahi, the wet and flooded, congested streets . . ."

Thirty-Three.

Looking into the peephole, I see her quietly step out of the elevator. She is talking on her phone. I open the door, welcoming her very cute face in.

"Hey asshole."

We hug. I squeeze one side of her lovely tush. She pinches mine. This woman smells like a Viennese garden. Today, her hair is bluish. All of her fingers are combing down her long hair as she is sitting down. Checking her phone in between.

The soft skin on this young woman is . . . is . . . is otherly. Pearly white, baby-textured and ready to make any man succumb to her desires. She is a hothouse.

She listens to my day's confessions.

"Did you show 'em?" she asks.

"Who?"

"The imbeciles you always complain about?"

"Not today. It was calm," I say.

"I got stared at, " she switches.

"Where?"

"At work . . ."

"The Ministry?"

"Where else . . . He sat there staring and gazing, confused and dazed. Salivating and wetting himself."

"Your beauty assassinated him, I bet."

Who can resist this gorgeous beast? I sure can not. I throw kisses all over her pearly white. Moist and satin to the touch, I can not stop harassing her skin. I can not resist her lips. Can not fight her nips.

That fucking Haras.

Her lips. Her vulva. Words are useless. My mind is wasted around her. She never resists, just opens up her legs with constant butter waiting to massage my phallus into submission. Her fingers continue combing down her hair. Her eyes perusing her phone.

"Get off the damn addiction!" I yell at her.

"Just checking my Snap and Insta accounts."

"For?"

"Leverage." She puts the phone down and gets on top for round two. Rhythms and rotations manifest. Sweat and the occasional ass spank heighten, not to mention a few nip squeezes and twists in between.

"What?"

She does not answer, but speeds up her gyrations. Laughing at my jealousy. At my old(er) age.

"What leverage?" I attempt while harassed by her pearly moisturizing cream.

Most of the posts are her alter ego. Photos curving her body, accentuating her eyes, bringing out her sexiness to the forefront. Bringing out her heat to a male infested horniness.

"Bitch, please!" rodeoing, giggling, slapping me cheek-to-cheek. "Close your trap, old man."

"OLD-ER."

"Enjoy the ride while you can, GRAND-PA." Fingernails casually combing her hair down. Eyes perusing her phone.

———

Shaheed Park.

Shaheed Park is one of Kuwait City's main attractions. I come here to try to get some peace because the space is new, the space is vegetated, because the damn place is spacious.

Lots of writing takes shape here. How ironic that I have to come to the center of Kuwait City, where it is the most crowded, to try to find solace in open and refurbished space. All around the park are buildings, and more buildings being built, standing like arrogant giants reaching up to God to be his best buddy. But, they also stand peering down at smaller structures with disdain. They look like they are in competition to see which is more architectural, more glitzy, more individualistic. To see which is more chauvinistic. They stand trying to show more of a special Kuwaiti than any other.

Rebuilt out of an aging, dancing water fountain park and other depilated areas, this park is the country's modern attempt at rebuilding, reusing and recycling developed parts to integrate it back into the quickly shifting waves of contemporary modernism.

It is superficially retreating the sickly.

Hide as much as possible by clothing it with a fresh haircut and shiny new clothes. Always keep up appearances.

Rarely treat and cure internal disorders.

The same was done immediately after the liberation of Kuwait. Mask everything to make people forget. Mask everything to make people look forward, forgetting the past, neglecting the fast moving present. And mask who suffered with materialism.

The Amreeki is waiting at a bench. He has his phone under a pack of cigarettes in one of his hands. Smokes have been his signature for as long as I have known him, tilting his head with his squinted eyes whenever he smokes. That is often.

What is with people and their tilts? Does tilting help with breathing?

We greet each other with handshakes, although he knows how to greet the Kuwaiti way of lightly kissing cheek-to-cheek.

Exhaustion is written all over his face. His blue eyes a little red, dark circles under his eyes, and an unshaven face put his tiredness at a ten from ten. Smokes probably sucked some of it out also. He is dead.

Luckily, it is the weekend.

The temperature is a cool 22 degrees Celsius. The sky is white, hazy. There is a little humidity and some wind but no dust, as is often the case. The winds are blowing from the east, from Iran's desert south. They are throwing around light paper and half smoked and put out cigarette butts.

We start walking one of the paths between imported plants. Imported ideas.

The Amreeki has been in the country since the early 80's. A defense contract brought his family, like many other families, to this tiny enclave to help develop it. He has been different compared to other Americans who have come and gone.

"I just don't have time anymore," he says about his teaching job. "Many of the kids just don't get art," he says about one of the many private American schools littering Kuwait. "These kids are not like the kids from the 80's," inferring he, I and other handful of international teens we grew up with, when Kuwait was putting down strong roots in the art and music world.

I ask how his art is doing in the marketplace. "People don't buy paintings here," he says as he smokes his cigarette very quietly.

"They don't buy books either. Hell, get them to read a few paragraphs first," I say.

"They'd rather take selfies in front of my paintings," describing the new generation of narcissistic social media addicts. Describing the new synthetic dolls who snap photos of themselves in hopes of being recognized as special art forms.

With tilted heads.

"They are cheap. They'd rather take photos of themselves in front of my art to gain fame for something they did not create."

"Kuwaitis are shrewd businesspeople," I tell him. "They try to negotiate things to death. It's in their blood. They know how to hustle."

The Amreeki starts talking about other artists. "Kuwaiti artists never struggled with rats in ruinous buildings from the bottom up. They don't know what struggle is," bending down to tie his shoes. He looks at me and says, "They copy each other," referring to the tilted faces that many artists have followed as a trend. "I'm tired of the tilting head paintings."

This is Kuwait. This is the Middle East. Most are not pure creations but copies of copies, like the illegal downloaded movies and music. This is why we are stuck, unlike our golden era when Arabs spread science and literature to many parts of the world. Now, we are too busy copying the West's ideas by bringing in their media, franchises, and Botox.

We stop at a sculpture depicting the martyrs who struggled during the Iraqi invasion a couple decades ago. Bricks are piled on top of each other, mounting to birds of flight. The art piece looks deformed in its symbolism, stuck between Arabism and a shifting wind of global, contemporary fluidity.

"Bisexuality is hip because of media," The Americano says about Kuwait's newest trend. "Copy and paste. Paste and copy. Copy and paste."

His face is a little turned off from this new mania that is changing Kuwait's social fabric because it can not control the flow of the young generation's need to test and break old customs. Homosexuality and bisexuality have always been rampant in Kuwait, but it was hidden. Now, it is in your face.

Come and get it is the new art.

A modern woman passes by and stares at The Amreeki. He smiles at her, but she returns with a repugnant look.

"Mo hillo face," he says to indicate the constipated facial look that many women pose when they are approached publicly, or when they are challenged to give an opinion on an issue, or when they simply just want narcissistic attention.

"Mo hillo" means "not good."

It seems we are constantly looking out for our own identity. Looking for our identity in the reprocessed. It appears we are constantly looking for any identity to identify consistently with.

Could it resemble how the majority in this tiny and young but wealthy country like to swap the old for the new, even though the old is relatively new?

Yes!

Kuwait has a young populace very good at starting dynamic projects, but it fails at preserving—maintaining— what it launches.

Service is key.

The service industry is weak. It is like how citizens are superimposed and tempted to marry early. They are lured by interest and tax-free social allowances to marry and have children, but rarely are young couples thoroughly advised in how to hold on to their marriage. So little is nurtured. Much more is spent on the dazzling new, making the recently aged replaceable. Making them upgradeable. Making them disposable.

This should alert the older authorities because if the young marry and procreate early with the older supremacy's subsidized wealth, the youth will create a larger demographic, which can overrun the older generation out of power. The older ones will vanish because of their own making.

It is already happening. If these kids and adolescents were ever to protest, the government would surely have a handful to deal with.

"That won't happen," many elders tell me with half a smile and half a frown, trying to hold on to their own appearance in the face of fear. "We'll just provide them with more and newer commercial entertainment."

Be very careful what you set in place. It might be you—us—who could be replaced by our own children.

It breaks when you force it. It breaks when you do not!

As we stroll through the park, so many exotic materials rise out of the flat arid desert. Granite and marble flooring, glass walls, encased rocks within hexagonal wires—oh, wires—and vegetative earth sprinkle among steel and iron casing. They are foreign architectural elaborations that are nesting and challenging the old status quo. They are preserving—covering—the desert floor with exotic textures and designs, organically sprouting from a once desert.

A park assembled by foreigners but credited to the locals.

The Ministry of Youth Affairs is helping to foster such a novel concept for supposedly Kuwait's youth. Kuwait's youthful future. The Minister and Undersecretary are young themselves. I assume they have been given these sorts of prestigious roles to boost confidence in their people to create diverse industries. Yet, one of the top positions at this ministry is run by a ruling family member, like so many other top positions, who was not voted in but appointed by another ruling member.

How does that boost confidence in us supposed commoners?

The Amreeki starts reminiscing about 80's Kuwait. He explains why the country was so attractive to him.

"I was untethered from Reaganomics."

He describes how the pressure of US politics back then stifled his sense of freedom. Even though he was a young kid, he knew what was going on.

"Other Americans in the 80's tried to bring their home with them," he says calmly. "They hated Kuwaiti culture, but now they miss it because of too many taxes, regulations and the feeling of constriction back in the States."

Kuwait's desert calm isolation made him feel serene. To him, the openness was "undisturbed and peaceful," showing how resetting oneself in a foreign land can land fresh perspectives.

A fresh happiness.

"Why in the hell did you always go after our women?" I interrupt. "What did you see in Kuwaiti women?" I ask him because he always had a mysterious fascination with the local women who were very prude and sexually unseasoned. Most of the ones he went after were virgins.

"I was attracted in what was not allowed," he says as we try to sit on a field of grass, but a security guard quickly comes and tells us treading on here is forbidden. There are not any signs forbidding anything.

"I always loved the pursuit of Kuwaiti women," detailing how they saw him as safe. The endurance, according to him, is in not giving up. That has been his goal all along. Not to give up was the reward. "They loved the chase," describing the Kuwaiti women who perhaps valued the chase more than the chaser.

The Kuwaiti women saw him, and may continue to see Americans, as exotic. Something and someone different may elevate sexual appeal. They may see Americans as mystical characters, thanks to Hollywood's plan to export films based on sheathed realities.

The Kuwaitiyat loved his freedom and continue to love freedom that takes them away from the shackles of tradition. They love what The Amreeki calls "The irresponsibility of superficiality." They were attracted to his non-materialistic freedom, pulled in by the slightly undefined.

The new.

I think they have been in love with the idea of freedom more than any person can actually provide them.

"So where do you live now?" he asks.

"Fintas."

He laughs. "Is the level of prostitution still high there?" he asks about when he recently lived there with his new Kuwaiti wife, before they had their son. "Chinese hookers were everywhere. They worked in the medical field, hired by their Kuwaiti contractors and pimped out to the shitty Americans," he elaborates about the military contracted men and women who reside on the front ends facing the Persian Gulf.

Shitty to mean they are not the images that diplomacy would ideally show to the world.

"How much do they go for?"

"30 KD. But they only approach Westerners. White men," he stresses.

"I guess you only go after brown women then?" I ask about the lightly tanned Kuwaitis he has had since who knows when.

"Damn, I couldn't even get those girls back then. How in the hell did *you* do it?"

He cracks up. He says he likes the build-up, but when the gorgeous lingerie and makeup are unveiled, the mystery is gone. Kuwaiti women are inexperienced to him.

They are not turn-ons anymore.

"But you married one?"

"I still love the chase," The Amreeki says while looking at a woman in niqab and abaya walking with five other women dressed in the same blackness.

The niqab is the face veil. The abaya, its body armor.

She actually starts to stare at him.

"When women are at traffic lights, their car waits a little behind when a local brown man is next to them," he describes. "But if he's white, they look and pull up."

"The American. The Amreeki who steals our women away, and in my own country," I jab at him. "That's balls!"

He goes farther and says that Kuwaiti mothers hit on him during teacher-parent conferences. "You get the occasional brush on the arms. It's like after the highs they get from shopping, then they move on to the next temptation."

Long garmented dishdashas stroll through the walkways. More abayas glide beside them. Joggers in head-veiled hijabs but body-tight running suits jog with a male companion leading them. Female repression still continues regardless of how flashy and enticing the clothes may be.

Children climb the imported and refined marble at most places that are dedicated to martyrs. The artistic representation is portrayed a little differently than what used to be done. Martyrs are now depicted a little more post-modernly than the typical Nasser era of Egypt's Middle East, the Arabism era which was portrayed more like Soviet era communism.

There is water glistening at central points in different areas of the park. Birds have come to settle. Butterflies to nestle. There are even colored fish pivoting around, in artificial ponds.

Space is stretched in this park. One can feel relieved for

a temporary time until they have to drive back home and deal with the suffocating traffic that the same authorities have not found a solution to.

Oh yeah, they are the same authorities that have caused the traffic mess to begin with.

After talking about the economics of the chase, The Amreeki starts discussing his wife. His new life. He seems to love how the old lady protects him in public to show ownership. But his art is his haven. In it, he feels detached from being defined as one nationality. As an American. Dwelling in his art, he finds that he is borderless, without a typical identity that is set by a government, set by traditional and social practices.

Through his art, he is the art itself.

Before he has to leave though, he has a puzzled look and asks, "How do I put the American in my son?"

Families who come to the park disperse from the tight traditions, testing their sense of freedom of movement. Testing their sense of purpose. They are breathing and unveiling much more human individuality to create purpose beyond government, and without a shroud of a doubt, beyond their own family plots to lead them into what they see as sensible traditions.

Balochi Pakistani men are wearing long white jamas, smock-frocks resembling robes that are worn all the way down to the heels. They look around in suspicious bewilderment, glancing at Arabs who are relaxing their traditions, in the midst of breathable oxygen.

Balls and bicycles are disavowed by park authorities. Barbecues and litter are circumcised. Young volunteers from local schools and universities help out comers by answering questions and giving directions.

There are not any signs forbidding anything.

But, cleaners in dark skin and uniformed, by one of the

few local companies that have been given tenders, sweep and mop the park. They are the forgotten slaves of modern times. They germinate right beside many of the park's exotic flowers and plants, appearing throughout the idealistic intentions of all the plants and fancy architecture.

Is this the new and brave Kuwait? I would have to investigate much more below the surface to see if there is anything hidden, if there is any other agenda at work.

There is always something hidden in this country.

Why? Because truth is too risky. Lies are much easier to deal with. Trusting authorities in this country would be a terrible mistake. We have seen them fail endlessly because of lies structured out of superficial promises. Desert Storm should have been a testament to that—an awakening.

Dishdasha-wearing security personnel patrol and courteously enforce park regulations. They are warding off corrupting the fostering and ecological biodiversity that is growing in the middle of giant glass windows and mountains of steel buildings in the surrounding skyline. It is as if the buildings are not suspicious anymore. As if finally Kuwait is regaining its footing, regaining its balance in a region festering with upheaval and warring ideologies.

I go to one end of the park entrenched in lush vegetation. Olive trees are spread out next to lined walk areas. Small evergreen shrubs with purple flowers— lavender—stick out underneath and next to the olive trees. There are even mint and alfalfa plants assembled and aligned with the others. Someone clearly takes good care of all of them. Someone clearly planned to have these specific plants in this area as symbols.

Good maintenance is necessary!

So is good symbolism!

After the fountains are twin golden towers, pillars erected to honor the ones who died during Saddam's 1990 invasion. They are immortalized through creative art, through expressive architecture, glorifying witnesses to Kuwait's nationalistic faith, but more to Islam and its principles. In this type of Islamic culture, martyrs are honored greatly.

Being one is a greater privilege.

The martyr sculpture shines goldenly, proudly recalling and immortalizing the souls who gave up their physical existence so that future children could understand why marble, steel, iron, glass, and much, much more plantation have risen from a deserted desert. Why so much has risen from an unused land, for the desert is never dead. Its secrets lie in the hidden energies that vibrate it into a Shangri-La gem. It lies right in the middle of business trade, car exhaust, traffic bustle, and endless layers of half-truths.

Sustainability. Kuwaiti style.

Artistic windows bulge out from elevated earth. Contemporary designs tease and play, and eventually calm each visitor's nervousness from driving. They breathe. They smell. They closely listen. They confidently exhale inhibited doubt.

There is a bookstore near the main entrance. It is tiny. Bookstores are so scarce. Barely anyone reads. Barely they read in English. Rarely does anyone write. Most of the books in the store are in Arabic, very thin in diameter, thickly large-fonted and over-spaced out by very young writers who write about limited romance and have strict deadlines to turn in stories to their local publishers.

It is all deliberate.

Few books are in English. Most are young adult fiction relating to dystopian themes. The clerk behind the counter is hypnotized by his phone. He does not even acknowledge me. According to one person I know at the Ministry of

Information, this major Kuwaiti bookseller takes original copies of bestselling books and has them cloned in India where the paper and printing is very cheap. To know what is original or not, I smell the paper when I open a book. Indian-printed paper has a repugnant smell unlike the smell of books that many of us have grown to whiffing and reading with pleasure. To whiffing that fresh book smell printed in the West.

Instead, so much is masked. More jumbled wires.

The powers that be do not want the majority of the population to read. They do not want them to think, especially critically. Shove cheap thrills, like smart phones and consumerism, down the populace's throats and hypnotize them into addiction. Keep them in social groups to monitor and control them. If behavior is controlled, it will set in a new movement as the norm.

That new movement is socialism.

It is coming throughout the world.

Many at the censorship board at the Ministry of Information are not qualified to know what to censor. Movies and books are examined at whim and then censored according to book cover and title. They do not know what the hell they are doing. The main reason to why they are not qualified is because the country has to put most citizens, graduates and otherwise, into government positions. Stronger salaries are in the public sector for Kuwaitis. Little oversight and a fraction of that in work ethic helps, like how employees skip work generously without deduction in wages or managerial oversight. Why? Because even managers abundantly skip work. A university student with a background in finance is suddenly part of a handful in the censorship committee censoring books of fiction, amongst at least half of the committee's overzealous Islamists. But when it comes to wasta that involves straight up cash, Islam and any other personal morals are thrown out of the window.

Hence, the repugnant cloned book smell.

Wasta is Kuwaitis' version of a silent revolt against the ruling family. Skip work and get paid at the end of the month like nothing happened. Higher managerial positions cover for the lower ranks, all covering one another's asses for the sake of a revolution, and for the sake of future connections.

It is not what you know that works in Kuwait. It is more of who you know.

The way most see it is that if the rulers are allowed to steal and thieve much of Kuwait's oil wealth and power, then so can the people who put them there.

Recently, an animated Walt Disney movie was pulled out of theatres because it contained homosexual acts of love. The pulling happened after the movie was allowed to air for a couple of days. Who censored it? The same Ministry of Information.

In Kuwait, homosexual acts are sinful and illegal. There is an actual law for it. Thanks to the two English newspapers in Kuwait, the gender fluid community is constantly propagandized and mocked, yet the same people in power partake in homosexuality and bisexuality with them. Who else would be providing visas to bring in the droves of Filipino gays into massage parlors and hair salons? To the underground parties? To government ministries as menial laborers?

It is so ludicrous that one of the normal headlines reads: "Over 200 homos, lesbians held in countrywide Net café raids." How and where exactly would a police station here hold that many supposed "homos" and lesbians? Would they be thrown in the tiny jail cells? If so, the police would probably have a grand old time with them, the perfect environment to exercise their true sexuality.

Or another headline refers to how Kuwait is developing a gay detector to keep LGBT expats out of the Gulf because they are "unfit."

Unfit?

Well, now! Who in the hell brought them in to begin with?

Would that gaydar include citizens, especially the arrest of top officials themselves?

Where was the censorship committee that was supposed to screen the Disney flick? They were probably eating the popular rice and meat dish called machbous and drinking liban. Buttermilk, liban, can sedate a grown muscular man into hibernation. Literally. It can knock out a person that strongly.

Or, the censorship board was out eating falafel sandwiches somewhere and drinking their Bebsi—Pepsi—not realizing or caring that they were supposed to be at work, screening content so that their own children would not be exposed to it.

Where is the oversight? Where is the rationale?

Intersecting with other wires.

My phone rings. It is an unknown number. "Yeah?" I ask.

"Hey asshole." 33 is at it again.

"How in the hell do you mask numbers?"

"Bitch, please!" she softly says. "Don't hustle a hustler."

"What do you want? I'm busy."

"Doing?"

"Gathering writing material."

"Cooking words on paper again?" She laughs with great confidence. "You need to get out more."

"I am out. You need to come over more. I hate driving in this madness."

"What are your lies about this time?"

"A gorgeous queen that no man can break."

"Talking about me?" her tempo calms down a little and her voice softens farther. "You and your beautiful words. When will you read them to me again? They always replenish my sins."

"Is that what does it to you? Simple words? Simple vocabulary?"

"My thighs are moist," throwing me off. "My inner earth needs servicing."

"Servicing?"

"Asshole, please! I'll be there at 5:30. Have the door ajar."

"Wallahi..."

She hangs up.

Walking near the Circle of Peace, there is a small crowd. The sun is setting. Much of the daylight has gone to sleep. I see a large video screen with ABOLISH ARTICLE 153 and women sitting in front of it, still and focused, like they are about to meditate to it.

What the hell is this article?

One young woman after another is reading poetry about some injustice that one man or another has supposedly committed. The young women are angry. Their words aggressive.

One of them looks like a university student. She climbs up on the small stage and starts talking about an invisible man. Her tall height and assertive verbs and tight adjectives squeeze at men in general.

Another shorter woman is stout. Her poetics are cunning, using clever stanzaic meter and rhyme. Her poetic soul is crying. Her words are bleeding out. They are thrown at this masculine world that has supposedly robbed her of living as an equal.

Both of them are wearing manmade hijabs.

A young man from the back row in the crowd of females walks up to me in the dark and asks, "What do you think of this movement?" seeing that very few males are around.

"Feminism?"

"No, the article?"

"I don't know it. What is it?"

"They want to abolish 153 which is the rite for men to kill their women if they shame their family."

"Shame how?"

"Infidelity." He says.

"So they hijack an old law to demand equal rights because they have a sexual need to cheat?"

He laughs loudly. A few women stare.

Wires.

"I didn't even know that exists here. Is honor killing even practiced with Kuwaiti families anymore? It's a law?" I push for any details. "I thought that was done in Pakistan or Afghanistan or some place."

He says no. He looks disinterested as well. He gets a phone call and vanishes.

I keep watching the females vent. The screen now has a soft voice asking, "Why do you want to hurt me?"

Who wants to hurt her? Which men? Are these women serious? They have put this much energy into blaming men for something most men do not even likely practice in this country. Where are the men who are battered by women in Kuwait? They do not have a parade bitching about it. They do not even report it. Why is that not looked at?

The abolishers seem to be campaigning for equal rights. I never understood the whole movement of gender-based equal rights. Men and women are of different biology, have different behaviors, have been exposed to different environments growing up.

Do they mean balance? Are they calling for more balance?

Shit! Give it to them. Let them go and work like we do, be raised to be unemotional robots, be called "men" at an early age when we are boys, and then be expected to take care of our females and children financially for life.

The guy comes back and just says one thing before catching another call and vanishing. "I wonder what would happen if we asked them to pay half for everything. Would they still want their equal rights?"

Brilliant!

It appears a small group of older women at this function are trying to bring Western feminism into the country. Backed by the American embassy, of course. I do not see how it will work if they follow Islam. A religion made and administered by men.

I leave the campaign and go to the farthest corner of the park. There is so much vegetation.

Shaheed Park, meaning the Martyr Park, is not simply a park. I believe it is trying to manifest the greatest human quality in each and every resident, regardless of nationality, power, or creed. Shaheed could be a testament to creative forces that are willing to sustain, nurture and exemplify the vegetation of human spirit. A testament to creative forces coming from different backgrounds and agendas in order for a communal space, a communal energy—vortex—to give rise to what Kuwait has to offer. What Kuwait is.

At least that is what is all portrayed throughout the park, most likely brainstormed, outlined, and written by foreigners.

But edited by Kuwaitis.

From its rulers to its manual cleaners, together they

have advertently, or inadvertently, created not a mere park but an ideology based on partnership, cooperation, respect, and admiration.

Although, twisted.

The moon sits glowing. Watching. Smiling.

So does Iran.

Urdu, Arabic, English, and other tongues are more loudly spoken, proudly demonstrated in front of each other at the park. They form a recipe of carefully knitted ingredients, each proud of its delicious heritage, yet more to feed harmoniously into a lifestyle that has been learning to cope as one, graciously.

Solar panels and sleek and refurbished steel designs are everywhere, and they are here to vertically and horizontally enlighten spirits so that residents can laugh and gleam as a community. This is the new Arabism in the context of internationality. Cosmopolitan in glitter. In sustainable humanity.

The reddening sky in the background is a crimson softness. The moon is brightening further. Enlivening. Glowing. It is grooming the human species for an identity searching for universal solidarity, searching for congruity.

I walk further into the park's intestines. Nearing one of the ends, the walkway descends, and along the walls that hold up the earth are faces. Military men, hijabed daughters and mothers, young sons and new fathers grace a descending wall commemorating their sacrifice during the war. Their nationalistic proudness stands out to a tiny but fierce country that repelled aggression, that fought off a hungry tyrant.

This is how they are portrayed at least.

This is how they are redeemed.

All the photos are planted in the walls in black and white, complexly lasered in monochromes, echoing the expensive grey and white marble floors that diagonally lead down to them. In pairs, human characteristics and traits, from mustaches to prescription glasses, to eyeliner and headwear, are lasered into the ceramic wall.

Mother to a son.

A young man to a father.

A Kuwaiti mirroring a Kuwaiti.

———

"Marhaba," The Haras says as "greeting" while I pass him to the elevator. He is crouched on a patio chair in his little room glaring into his phone while sucking like a blowjob pro into a shisha. He has the front door slightly open to screen unwanted guests who do not pay a toll.

Kuwaitis are forbidden to rent apartments by law if they are single.

Every other nationality is allowed to, though.

In my own country I feel unwelcome and unwanted. The government makes it hard for even Kuwaiti divorcees to rent. I am discriminated by my own people.

This is why The Haras wants a toll because quite a few in the building are single Kuwaiti renters, but they do not live in the apartments full-time. And if a woman is brought up for illicit practices, then a hefty toll is administered. Illegally.

The Troll keeps a tab on all who wish to pass through. If there is any deviance, a toll is slapped on.

How ridiculous.

I was fortunate enough to use wasta I never intended on using to get my place. I called up a real estate broker friend of mine, and he made things work to get in.

Just. To. Get. In.

Millennials and their one-worded sentences.

It was not for free. Nothing is ever for free here. I had to illegally buy him a few bottles of alcohol for services rendered. I had to exercise an illegal transaction to help another illegal transaction take place.

If The Haras catches women coming up to see me, a tax is applied. Getting into the apartment was one story. Women coming up is another. If I choose not to play, the Kuwaiti landlord is called and a shit storm ensues.

Wallahied wires.

The Haras responds with "Ahlan, Basha," puckering up to mean "Welcome, Pasha."

Turkey sure bastardized Egyptian Arabic.

"I just washed your car." He clearly wants any bakhsheesh—tips—he can get for services already tipped.

Haras and the English word harass. Damn, could it be? Could the two words from very two different languages mean the same thing, which in this case means a building guard who harasses his tenants for as much cash as possible?

"When are they going to clean the ac filter?" I throw at him.

"Wallahi . . ."

Right. On. Cue.

Millennials!

––––––––

The Haus.

I am waiting downstairs for her to invite me upstairs to her apartment. I finally get a message with the apartment number. I sense she is a little paranoid because we have never met before in person even though we know of each other.

We greet at the door with a hug and a light cheek-to-cheek kiss, without truly using the lips to kiss. It is a typical greeting with someone you are strangers with or one you see too much of. Or one who does not want her makeup to smudge.

The unclearness fits most of what happens in the country.

Near the front door is an electrician pulling out and testing wires. Two females await us in the living room. One looks like a bulldyke, boyish short hair and thick bones hold up her personality. Her voice is deep, masculine. No makeup is glossed over her face.

The other female seems to be her part-time lover. More feminine, elegant, fit, curvy, and fluent with how she maneuvers her hair, body, lips, and glazed smile.

They both have lovely youthful smiles. I feel proud of them for some reason. Not so much for being homosexual, or heterosexual, or bisexual, or any other sexuality, but for resisting older traditions they had little choice in making. They are the new Kuwait. The new dynamism that old Kuwait can not alter or stop.

Kuwait is certainly changing, coming out, flexing its gender-fluid identity much more publicly than just a few years back. The country is waking up because of these young, more individualized energy forces. They are the backbone. Their numbers outstrip older adults, if not throughout the entire Middle East. They should be able to show their creativity and passion as much as possible.

The Haus—the host—asks what I would like to drink in a Kuwaiti dialect. By drink, she means alcohol.

"Indee vudka. You want, habibi?" she says in a badliya, to which the Arabic part means, "I have vodka."

Badleyat is the Arabic plural form meaning the changes

between things. In this case, it refers to language interchangeability. It is a mix of Arabic and English, clearly showing how the onslaught of English—American—is changing the country's lingual history. It is also a very clear indication of how it is killing off the Arabic language's rich heritage.

"Habibi," or even the feminine "habibti," denotes "my love." Habibi is popularly used in most phrases in Arabic, so much so that it is a term to soften circumstances; soften hostilities. It is a term to soften vulgarities. Soften deceit, both self-practicing and otherwise.

I call her The Haus, just as the word means, because she seems to juggle so many crafts with brilliant artistry. From singing, to modeling, to launching herself as a businesswoman, The Haus has nailed the art of entertainment into business from what appears to be her own interpretation in Kuwait, the Middle East, and surely soon, the rest of the world. She is on a path of fame built on self-expression. And, she is still in her twenties.

How can I deny such integrity, such artistry, such brilliance? I can not. I will not. Instead, I welcome it.

The two young women start interrogating me about my writing profession. Somewhere in between, love as a theme springs up, teasing and testing my own interpretations of what I have come to know about the word, experience, and without doubt, the abstract euphoria it generates whenever I am in it.

Whenever I am out of it.

The Haus comes back with a crippling vodka and lemon cocktail. I guess she wants to open my true intentions up very quickly. As she ought to. I am sure many men have tried to score her for one thing, and one thing only. Dimples that complement large, encompassing lightly colored eyes, and a healthy bosom rack that is proportioned so symmetrically well to her Arab curves, make her a knockout. Oh, how her curves spellbind.

The women are simple in their verbal architecture. Words are poised simply. Their ideas are delivered a little more complexly. Watching them talk about one subject or another is amusing.

I am a man. I am a minority in their midst.

They are mostly conversing with one another, exposing one love relation or another. So much is about love. So much faith is placed on something that is so abstract. I can not grasp how they yearn, even though so much pain may have obtruded them, for the same thing again and again. They talk as if they are tourists residually moving in phases of love's multiple definitions; experiences. Experiential.

The Haus glances from time to time, examining my reactions to her and her guests, her friends. The Russian assassin of a drink does little, thanks to experience. Thanks to many years of experience. Many years of aging wisdom.

The electrician finally gives The Haus a rude, steep bill for little work. She pays the man without complaining in front of him. But, as soon as he leaves, she unleashes a controlled protest in the most gorgeous and subtle Arabic way. It is slightly manly, cursing a man's deceptive practices, which is a deeper and more symbolic curse to man's general sense of overpowering women into self-censored repression. The way she raises her eyebrows, squints her eyes, bobs her head, and squeezes together her fingers tells me that. It is the universal language for: An eye for an eye.

She increases the volume of the TV that she has had on with Arabic and English videos singing about one newly found love to another, one lost love or another. The women get up and start gently dancing, not caring about a man in their presence.

I guess I do not intimidate them.

I guess I am invisible.

Good.

A badliya dance, which is belly dancing and hip hop, take over the room, until The Haus changes the music to a Moroccan, very stylishly traditional Berber song. A male voice starts the song with a slow aching voice, almost like a Muslim call of prayer, but the dialect is thick, grabby. The other two dim the lights, light up some candles, chug some of their stiff drinks, and sit down to spectate The Haus's singing and dancing.

They know what is coming.

The voice through the TV continues to heighten, climaxing and stretching chords, pulling the young women to make faces of pleasurable agony. The Haus, though, begins testing her own voice along with the video's, but it is her body which is singing much more. She makes it move with fluidity, sharply tilting her torso from one corner to the other.

The wanted type of tilts!

One of her arms moves in torturously sedative swirls, bringing them forward to the very tips of her fingers, where her eyes initiate a round of tantalization, as if her various body figures are aiming to hypnotize, as if they are all inviting into the deep recesses of her womanhood. She is luring in eyes into the very dark portions of a woman's eroticism. Mysticism. Definite Arab exoticism.

The dark lined eyes are kissing at me. They are calling. They are luring me into her world, one that has not been explored and discovered properly.

This Arab woman is a vortex, waving at and undulating to make me lose my masculine power—my male-oriented sway. She is tempting the man in me to step out, to perhaps let go of myself and surrender to her tender artistry of softening everything that comes in her path.

How can I resist her call? Why would I want to hold on to myself in the face of such striking temptation?

Her eyes are sexually drunk and drinking me out. The fingers are tugging against her quivering breasts. She, overall, is dancing into submission by belly dancing at my desires, at my control. At my man-infested world where we as men think we are in control, when we are clearly not. We are only deluding ourselves.

The other two suddenly yell out "Allaah," taking God's name in complimentary vain.

———

Skin.

"Get in."

"What?"

"I said, get in!"

"Why?"

"Get your Filipino face in here and you'll find out."

I get in and he peels out, almost hitting a few parked cars. He does a U-turn cutting off other cars that have waited legally before speeding over bumps and almost ramming a truck at a roundabout.

Those Brits and their street terms.

We finally get on the intersection, and he floors it on the emergency lane.

"Whose car is this?"

"Company car. Shut it and open the glove compartment."

"Why?"

"You and your damn why's. Open it. There's a minibar in there."

Small bottles of Johnny Walker Red, a few gins, and a vaporizer are crammed together. There are no registration papers, or any papers of any kind.

"Hand me the vape, will ya?"

Dense vapor comes out of his mouth, and he blows them straight into my face. The car's interior is swamped with still smoke.

"How are you handling divorce?" weaving in and out of cars.

Some guy honks in protest, but Skin rolls down the window and throws out an American middle finger at him.

Smoke remains lingering.

The other driver loses it and chases us between cars. Skin does some hard brakes in front of him and accelerates, teasing and scaring the other driver to give up.

"It's been shite."

He laughs at my British version of crap.

"How's the single life?"

"Alhamdulillah," he says with an Egyptian accent, thanking Allah.

I can barely see him with so much smoke trapped in the car.

"Space is important. I need my alone time. Having a woman constantly around would kill all that."

Agreeable.

"Why would any man," he continues, "want to be stuck with the same woman for so long? It's not natural. My life has gotta be better than the misery most couples endure."

What a point to make. I have been waiting for this type of bluntness for so long.

"The guy has to got to work, come home, be bombarded by noisy little shits, and throw most of his money on a woman he can't upgrade. If he tries, he will be an indebted slave for life, paying off the house that should have belonged to him, paying a warped sense of alimony and paying off the kids' school fees. My life is better than what you went through," he says like a prophet.

"Asshole!"

"It all ends," he says.

Dense vapors are blocking more of my vision. I can barely see the road in front.

"Habibi, nothing lasts forever."

Skin has a point. His body is supertoned for a 40 something year old. Never married. Never had kids. He migrates from one woman to another. And they all seem to be much younger than him. He used to be so skinny growing up. Now look at him. I chug down one of his Reds. "How'd get these?

"Some Thai airline hostess I met heading back from Bangkok smuggled them off the plane."

"Aren't they called attendant these days? Some say hostess is demeaning."

"Like many of the misandrist women you meet?"

"Misandrist?"

"The intellectual feminists you love to fuck with. The ones who call us misogynists."

"That's the term?"

"Yeah. You haven't heard of it because men don't bitch like women. I bet you haven't heard of womanhandle either."

"It doesn't exist."

"It does now. We're womanhandled by mothers. Sisters. Girlfriends. They bring us into this world when we barely understand how to search for hope, and then they take us out of life just when we think we have hope."

"Was the hostess any good?"

"The hostess and I Mile High Clubbed on a few trips to and fro. She loves using hand gesture emergency procedures in the toilet anytime the plane goes through turbulence."

"You're the epitome of asshole! I suffered for many years settling down while you roam the skies hosting a hostess."

"Oh, she hosts *me*, habibi. There's lots of servicing, habibi. Lots. "

"Don't you get enough of that shite over there? Drinking? Whoring? Sinning?"

More of his vapors are blown, drenching me into submitting to an issue he views as futile.

"Hell, no! Most of the guys I meet over there are running away from their kids. Their dull wives. Unlike you who bitches by writing about it."

"Marriage can be good. I miss family life. I miss my kids, man. You think I want to be single? I don't! I used to cook, clean, and play with my kids. That was my world. Simple but full of love."

"But then?"

"But I wasn't needed anymore by the wife. I was treated like an invisible machine. I was emotionally neglected. Spiritually rejected." I try to close the glove compartment, but it keeps falling back down slowly. "Does anything work properly in this country?"

"Inshallah, habibi," reaching over, pulling out one of the gin bottles and jabbing it at me.

"Husbands become second class when there are children. And now I live illegally as a divorcee with cracks all over the apartment. The kitchen water faucet drips. The toilet has no seat. Wires dangle outside the window. I have to deal with assholes like yourself all over the road. Assholes like you who travel so easily all over the world."

Skin laughs and blows more smoke into my face, smokescreening my thoughts. My sanity. He drags the vapes and holds them before saying, "The Kuwaiti government gives us full-ride scholarships to study in the U.S. and they expect us to uphold a 3.0 GPA and finish in 4 years. That's also with a stipend so we don't get any work experience from a first world country. Then when we come back to this rich but third world country, they tell us to slow down and not work so fast."

"Give me that damn vape." I yell at him. "Millennials and their vapes."

Suddenly we are back on my street. He pulls in front of the apartment building and says, "Get out. Get the fuck out, Flip! I have to go back to work and punch in before traffic hell turns loose."

I quickly get out.

Skin floors it, laughing and peeling away with a smoked interior.

I park outside an Arabic restaurant on what is dubbed Restaurant Street. There are no places to eat inside because such places are bed or living-roomed sizes, usually shoved just under apartment buildings. Stacks of cars are parked out of formation under and in front of the buildings because very little planning was thought of during the formation of the infrastructure back in the 80's. Kuwait still has not gentrified much of the back areas of Fintas.

Much of this area is a ghetto reserved for the foreign workers of Kuwait. They are the people who are used to clean, cook, and service the Kuwaitis, but they are hidden from sight in such places otherwise. In this overly concentrated slum, residents are primarily Islamists who have been pushed out of wealthier areas of Kuwait City.

Egyptians, Bengalis, Syrians, Indians, and Bedouin Islamists live side by side with American and British teachers and military personnel.

It is a firecracker with a short fuse.

Take away and drive away are thus the only options at most restaurants. Most of the employees taking orders are Egyptian. Classifying people according to nationality in Kuwait is important because it demonstrates how things operate. It is a caste system few care to talk about because in Islam castes do not—should not—exist.

I honk and one of the men comes out. He says without asking that I want a kebab meal.

I just look at him. Yes, I was here a few days back, but I am quite sure he did not take my order.

"I don't forget a face," smiling. "You usually order kebab," finishing my thought for me.

I wait a few seconds before saying, "Yes, I do."

"I never forget a face," he stresses. "Even after a year, I'll still remember a person's order," he says in Egyptian Arabic, in a quick dialect where the consonants are masculine and the vowels feminine, making it difficult for many Kuwaitis to follow. Add a few head movements to stress the consonants and add a few facial expressions, like wide smiles and gleaming eyes to soften them with vowels, and an Egyptian looks and sounds like an actor on stage. It is worth the entertainment.

He is leaving to give my order to the kitchen.

"I want a chicken kebab meal," I yell at him to come back. He returns and fumbles with his white uniformed paper hat, and says "Inshallah" to mean it is coming right up, if God wills it.

"Inshallah!" This is the most used term in the Arabic language regardless of which dialect or country one is in. Although Arabs love to cause friction amongst each other, they seem to always use "Inshallah" to get out of it. The mess Arabs create is normally larger than the "Inshallahs" that are given. Like the apartment buildings and restaurants in this area.

For Kuwaitis, they are excellent at starting a project, yet rarely do they know how to maintain and service it efficiently. The service industry needs to catch up with the likes of Dubai.

"Inshallah" is the best way to get out of one's own mess. And if the mess potentially leads to violence, "habibi" or "habibti" is added either before or after "Inshallah."

"Inshallah habibi!" I hear the same Egyptian scream pleasantly to a grown Kuwaiti male—at least I think he is Kuwaiti—who has just parked next to me in his humongous SUV. The supposed Kuwaiti starts blaring out words in a macho, muscular tone of voice, in all likelihood not in his natural tone.

Most Kuwaiti men use deep-throated bass tones to project power, especially when they talk with non-Kuwaitis.

Or women.

The guy looks like most Kuwaiti men in their adolescence, a goatee peeling down his face toward a stretched out beard, hidden by a white headdress that acts like a curtain on the sides of the face, which is tied in to flow like the long dishdasha.

The dishdasha is beautiful to look at. Wearing one though is hard. There are too many layers, causing way too much discomfort. Plus, it looks bland. Although I seem to get much more respect when I wear it, it is not worth the effort of constantly dry-cleaning it and worrying about creases.

I guess such men think it makes them virile-looking. They all look the same. Downtown, I see flocks of them talking in the same intonation, constantly adjusting their headdress, persistently congratulating themselves—by being condescending—to further their fraternal machismo. Uniforms are meant to be worn because one has to, such as in schools, companies, factories, hospitals.

Not leisurely!

It is a typical craze in Kuwait. When one of them starts a trend, most of the others herd behind. Individual uniqueness is a strange phenomenon here.

Thank the egalitarian school system and Islam for that.

My food should be out in about ten to fifteen minutes. While waiting, I turn on my emergency lights. I rarely turn them on while waiting for food outside such a place, but there are too many cars cram-parked, so I do not want to take chances if cars driving by get too close.

And they love to drive close here.

In a country with one of the highest car accidents in the world, I would rather not take chances and push on some emergency lights.

Large and sparky European public buses fly by. They are like moving red buildings—but rectangularly muscular. I watch through both the side and rear view mirrors. This exact crossing is waiting for an accident to happen. I feel it. It is in the air. It is in how the place was designed. In how it was poorly and corruptly planned.

The Egyptian is waving a group of Bedouin kids to leave the front of the restaurant after receiving their take away order. Few of the taller boys are wearing traditional dishdashas. Few of the other younger and much smaller boys in jeans and shirts are picking on the larger boys, trying to tease and grab their food. The big kids whip the little ones away with their hands, and they all hurry and vanish in between the parked cars.

A bright red double-decker flies by, breaking often to

cars pulling out of the buildings and Asian walkers trying to cross, or Asians actually trying to catch the bus. There is a bus stop just in front of the crammed apartment buildings. So much metal—cars—is parked around the faded blue pole sign that it makes one wonder how a human is expected to wait anywhere around it. There are no sidewalks around, either.

Most of Kuwait does not have sidewalks. I guess human worth, if you are not a Kuwaiti driving a lavish car, is not valued so much. And whenever there are sidewalks, they are normally wide and abandoned. Many pedestrians choose to blatantly walk on the street rather than the wide empty walkways.

Kuwaitis do not ride the public buses. They do not have to. Gasoline is subsided so cheaply that it is actually cheaper than bottled water, even if they recently raised gas prices.

One guy at the stop is waving like a drowning man for the bus driver to stop. The bus driver delays his stop at about 100 feet ahead of the bus stop, but he stops on the fast lane of the two-lane road, causing Asian-driven taxis and other motorists to honk in a symphony of unwanted noise.

This is the norm.

The man finally gets on and the bus accelerates, pulling and breaking its double-decking weight to its next destination.

It is ok. Gas is cheap.

The hierarchy corrupt.

Continuing to wait, I roll down the windows to get fresh air. I see a young woman coming out of the building in front of the restaurant and bus stop. She is walking quickly in between the stuffed cars, passing by closely, looking down to the pavement and probably fake-talking on her mobile phone.

Most women ghost talk on their phone when they sense discomfort. Usually, it is caused by too much testosterone staring at them. Men love to use their eyes as weapons in the Middle East, especially if they are gazing at women.

Women love to veil themselves. Yet, many seem to also love to show more of themselves, inviting prying eyes into their secret world.

It is an inshallah of a falafel of a mess.

As the woman passes, I hear a male voice coming out of her mouth. She is clearly a young man. She looks at me quickly with male eyes—hard and unrelenting gapes. S(h)e has clearly shaved, so remnants of a close shave are visible.

Why is it not a surprise anymore? So much homosexuality, bisexuality and now parasexuality is rising in Kuwait, much like what started a while ago in the States.

I look back at the building where s(h)e came from and notice a spa sign peering out from the first floor.

Umhmm.

Spas are segregated, but girly-looking men either work at such establishments to serve the massive amounts of men who are well-respected married fathers in public but identity-bending freaks when they frequent dark spas for massages and who knows what else.

They can not be blamed. Men are raised in segregated public schools. Having males most of your pubescent and adolescent life side by side with you must breed homosexual, if not otherwise, tendencies. Once that is established, as it is in many prisons around the world, then classifications start to happen. The soft men serve the gorilla-acting men. Gorillas serve them back by submitting to their softness. It is a clear but organized mess.

Much like the country's corruption, double-standards, and "Inshallah!"

Still waiting for my food. A Filipina-looking grandmother tries to cross the street after shopping at the Coop nearby. She is exhausted. Step by slow step, she crawls to her destination. I turn to the other side to see if my order is being delivered yet. Suddenly, I hear a massive thump, and a body rolls forward on the street. Only feet away. The body is of a young Asian man. The grandmother starts screaming. The true meaning of Inshallahs and a few other suffix ending -allahs come out from many directions.

One of the new red public buses hit the Asian pedestrian. I immediately move my car further down the road, away from less crammed cars. Getting out to see if the man is not dead, many Asians group around the injured. They block the view. A few head veiled mithajabas try to console him. The Egyptian waiter brings out a chair for him to sit on. A short fat Kuwaiti in a grey and white school uniform walks to one of the Asians who is filming the injured man with his mobile phone and starts kicking him, saying, "Are you insane? A man just got hit and you are videoing it?" He asks the video-taker for his phone and demands an ID from him.

There is no way in hell this Kuwaiti-sounding punk is a cop. He is too fat and too young. He just knows that most menial laborers are illiterate, so he is taking advantage of the situation.

A real cop finally shows up. More traffic is backed up to the all-around crammed area. It is a quick gentrifying of already gentrified gentrification.

I am so disgusted at witnessing violence. Not only by a bus driver who is incompetent for driving too fast, but by how the injured man was handled, how a young deceitful Kuwaiti used further violence by yelling and kicking another Asian, and how my food is taking so damn long to get. I just want to get the hell out of here and go to a nearby park to eat in peace and quiet.

Violence in any form turns me off. Literally! I close down. I do not talk much. I withdraw. Open space is where I go where people do not steal the space I have made for myself.

I need space. My age has earned it.

The food is finally brought, and I swiftly leave to the park. My face is numb. Disappointed. Violence begets violence, I know that. It is an energy force which once started continues to enlarge and expand. I know that because I have experienced it so many times. The first Persian Gulf War made me see humans at their worst. There was so much senseless stealing, raping, and killing. And for what? Invisible borders? For a black liquid called oil? Abstract power?

At the park, there is an empty shaded table near a fenced soccer field with kids playing in it. What are kids doing out here during school hours?

Weak oversight and accountability!

Like infrastructural planning and maintenance!

Street cats show up at the smell of my food.

Damn! Can I not have my space?

I will eat in my car. There is just too much disturbance. Right as I am leaving, I hear loud male voices from the soccer field. They are the same kids from the restaurant earlier, beating up one kid. They all run around me trying to punch and kick a tall Egyptian kid. His face is registering the same type of disgust I have had. He is running away very fast.

I yell in Kuwaiti to the oldest bully. He stops running and faces me asking, "What?" in a violent pose. But, seeing I am bigger and perhaps fitter than him, he leaves me alone, laughing at his smaller kids in his gang who are chasing the Egyptian kid away.

Disgusting!

Disgusted!

Violence begets violence.

Eating in the car, the food is tasteless; unenjoyable. I monitor the kid gang. They are throwing shoes and sandals at each other and laughing about it.

Shameless!

An older and overweight American couple walks past them with their faces pointed to the ground. They are probably used to seeing this. They are most surely used to feeling disgusted. How do I know they are American? Long shorts on the man, pulled up socks and 80's sneakers and an oversized T-shirt reading, TENESSEE VOLUNTEERS—a college football team that many may not have heard of, including by a good amount of Americans. The woman— the wife— has a large hair-do, puffed at the sides. It almost resembles a mullet for a man but ballooned, wavy and longed out.

Some never leave a golden era.

Some choose to be stuck.

Once I finish the food, I drive to a nearby shopping mall to catch a movie. An American film, more Hollywood stories trying to teach the rest of the world about ethics. About terrorism. About themselves.

I park the car away from everyone.

Space.

Space is important. I can breathe when there is ample space. Otherwise, I lose control. I lose myself.

I take out a few notes and some coins. The wallet is left behind. It is too weighty. I do not want a bulky ass protruding out of my jeans when I have to climb sets of stairs and escalators. The phone is turned off and tucked away with my wallet under one of the back seats.

A woman with a facial veil parks next to me. She comes

out and motions with her fingers to roll down the window. She asks if I know how to turn off her lights. "Inshallah," I tell her.

I go and turn off her emergency lights. "Is that what it was," she says, smiling out of her cracked eyes. She thanks me and goes into the mall.

Strolling through different levels of the mall, I hear a female shout coming out of one of the shops. I pass near it and see a head veiled woman holding on pantyhose screaming to two Filipina employees, who are also wearing the hijab. From what I can gather, the woman is demanding a refund for an alleged defect. The Filipinas stand together pointing in broken Arabic to the receipt that says: NO EXCHANGES OR REFUNDS.

Many small shops use that policy here. Quite a few of their products are knockoffs.

Very little oversight leads to much more dishonesty.

A male security rushes over, but he has to stand at a distance, not knowing how to handle such a situation because if he gets too close, the woman may yell rape. If he does nothing, then the shouting will continue.

It sounds like the restaurant and the dysfunctional planning of all the buildings surrounding it. Including people's shenanigans.

I just want to watch a movie. Why is it so hard just to get to the theatre? Why must so much violence keep coming my way?

I finally get to the cinema, which is located on the top floor. When my turn comes up to buy a ticket, the Filipino behind the glass screen says this theatre is for families only.

Bosphorus.

Outside in the residential area of Salaam in South Surra, I greet her with cheek-to-cheek kissing. Houses are tight. They can barely breathe. Barely exhale. The kisses are shallow. Pretentious. It is part of the culture. We move downstairs into the basement. Expats, as they like to call themselves, are sitting outside in the tiny patio area smoking cigarettes and cigars in over 110-Fahrenheit heat. A table of locally made entrepreneurial food inside near the door is flashier than the taste itself.

Presentation is key.

Greater effort is placed on the exterior than substance. It perfectly shows the ins and outs of Kuwait. Of probably most of the world.

In the back next to the swimming pool is a large sign reading, 60 IS NOT OLD IT'S CLASSIC. Someone lied. Old is old. Body parts decay. Senility creeps in. Death is waiting. But a bar in the kitchenette buried under the stairs will soon spruce all that up.

Bosphorus quickly introduces me as "Nobody," as I like to be named, to a few Europeans. "He's a writer. He's working on his fourth novel."

Presentation is key.

One Arab-looking woman with green tattoos on her arms introduces herself. "I'm Nada." She has short androgynous hair, colorful contacts, lots of skin.

I respond, "I'm Nobody."

"Nobody? That's your name?"

"Yes."

Hands are lightly shaken with more couples. Eyes smiling. Lies flourishing. People are costumed up for Halloween. Am I missing something? It is early October. People are dressed in Austro-Bavarian dirndl and lederhosen clothing, traditional and simple country attire.

Why are they dressed like this in a desert with treacherous heat?

Most seem married. Most of the men are American. Their women naturalized Americans, probably fell for the trap of the American dream. Expats marrying other expats. All imports in an exported country.

The men look worn out. Defeated. Long stiff drinks in their hands. They are positioned slightly behind their women. They are out of shape. Given in to pussy. They are most likely whipped by yakking.

Most of the women, though, look fitter. They look glancier. They seem to want to explore new adventures with men who not only look good, who have proficiency to verbalize words into poetry, but also the knack to sexualize their vanity. They want to import some man's genuine, neoteric ideals while exporting themselves through varying shades of identity to different cultures. As fresh residual tourists.

Love is a bitch. Many women prefer to be loved. Fewer love blindly.

Someone is playing Boney M music off a smartphone in the background. Whoever switched it on must be European or influenced by Euros. Boney M was a Euro-Caribbean disco trio from the 70's. The main singer wore his huge Afro parted.

That is right, parted.

That was a sight. Guts! That must have taken some Anglo-produced hair containment to tame. Add in the butterfly-collared shirts and tight bell-bottomed pants, and walla. You have the Euro adaptation of one of the Jacksons.

One of the expat wives is Latin. Chilean, I believe. She is wearing a body tight black dress. Curves. Long and soft thick hair runs down to her round ass. She is probably in her 50's; her face is caught up by stress-driven wrinkles.

Her body is not catching up, though. It is casually waiting in her 30's. We dance a few songs to some 70's and 80's American disco. We are salsa-ing and rhumba-ing during choruses, but making sure her American husband does not get angsty if we were to draw any closer.

"What are your books about," she asks while her body slithers to the refrains.

"Corruption," I whisper softly in one of her ears. "Sometimes truths."

Yeah, I am no exception. Mess, is what I am. Where is my venom? I belong with these people.

Bosphorus comes to ask if I am hungry. She is a caterer. Giving oozes out of her in justly ways. Bringing food. Bringing drinks. Bringing her horniness when it is least expected.

"How were your travels?" she asks.

"Full of honest lechery."

I call her Bosphorus because she epitomizes the strait that connects the Black Sea with the Sea of Marmara and separates Europe from the Anatolian peninsula of western Asia. Istanbul is located at its south end. Its currents move southerly. Undercurrents like eddies and swirls astutely work against the main flow. That is her. That is this woman. This hotelier. She holds a key to endless taboo stories wherever she hotels guests.

"Wanna shoot a few tequilas down?" she throws. Taking my hand and heading to the kitchenette, she assembles lemons and limes in a small round tray while coating shot glass rims with salt. And she does it with incredible grace.

In this case, presentation shows so much.

I met this woman at an empty coffee shop in the new hotel where she works. Examining the opulent décor of the shop, and the many young cosmetic women snapping away photos in tilted-face formations, Bosphorus saw me writing the experience down in an old notebook.

That notebook by itself is a story of stories.

She gave a smug face in my direction. She seemed to understand my perceptions. I eventually went up to her and talked about writing. It led to a rare tour of the hotel. Eyes lit, words seeped, smiles enlarged, then bodies awakened.

Every affect and effect has led to this party.

Beautifying sights and tastes are her cornerstone. Succulent limes, finger foods to the side, gorgeous dish artistry and that continual smug smile make her alluring. Before we can shoot the tequila down, a clean-cut young man in formal attire shows up and starts talking to her in an agglutinative vowelized language. It sounds like a European Romance language mixed with Arabic and Persian. Soft and hard-sounding words are meshed together seamlessly. It is poetic. Infectiously addictive. Turkish.

It is so similar to the Bosphorus' contrasting currents; swirling and swaying. The sounds tug and push away as if they are hypnotizing the listener with vivid syllables and vowel harmonies.

He listens to her like a simple soldier taking orders. Mechanically, he takes out, puts down, and finesses the bar counter with olive oils and garnished veggies in animal formations and beachy alcoholic drinks.

"I helped him escape being drafted from military service," Bosphorus whispers just before the first shot is downed. "The only way to be pardoned in Turkey is to rape gays," her face stretches long but holding on to that smugness.

The actual 60 IS NOT OLD IT'S CLASSIC birthday boy finally shows. At the bar. Rugged hands are stretched out, shaken and released immediately in a militant fashion.

"This is a local author," Bosphorus eddies out.

"Tequila your preference?" he asks her.

"It's for the writer."

"Got to kill myself the most illegal way while dealing with the insanity of this country," I calmly let out.

"The bar's all yours," leaving to meet and greet other guests.

"How'd you get all these bottles?" I ask.

"DIP-LO-MATS," syllabizing secrecy in his pronunciation. "They all sell and profit from it as a side business."

"Oh yeah? How much?"

"They make much more than their ambassadorial jobs, that's for sure." Without caring who hears, "I pay 750 KD for a carton of Black Label."

Shit! That is about 2500 American. Shit!

How would anyone get off that sort of addiction?

Bosphorus gets into a hoteliering vignette. "Some of the big subjects are merely a masturbation," she says about the hotel meetings in Istanbul, London, Washington D.C., Kuwait, or whenever management wants her to fly to Chicago. "Men trying to boss everyone around with insignificance and their pricks," clasping in her right hand and motioning it vertically. "It's always a slow jerk off. "

"How do you amuse their insignificance?"

"Many layered smiles, dimples, and yes sirs as I lay out lavish food and their favorite alcohols," pointing to the food that she prepared me.

She loves to pamper with delicate food presentations. Fingered foods.

Yes, finger-ed.

Vivid colors. Mesmerizing but confusing tastes. All the while her prey is divulging information about himself while she takes notes to climb up the same ladder men have greatly tried to keep out of the reach of women. Flood them with pleasures to usurp their power.

What a true Bosphorus.

She is The Boss who likes to softly boss men around publicly but submit to them holily privately.

"Are you taking notes tonight?" she asks while winking.

"Always!" taking down the next shot. "Mental notes."

"Will this fiasco be in your next book?"

"Depends on how much hilarious decadence there'll be."

"Tell me something. Why do Kuwaiti women put on so much makeup? At every wedding we've hosted at the hotel, the women are covered head to foot with luxury. So much extravagance."

"It's the Gulf. Much is hidden behind shallow clothes and abundant makeup. They don't know how to be barren. They don't know how to be 'free,' as Westerners like to think of themselves. It's the patriarchy here that's done that to them, but they are slowly breaking off and away from it. Kuwaiti women are an enigma to themselves."

Two young Kuwaiti women come in and start dancing. One has short hair. The other has long. Both of them are wearing black dresses with high heels. Both have cosmetic faces.

Bosphorus sees me looking at them. They begin dancing while munching on food.

The shorthaired one comes to the bar and steals the tequila bottle and starts downing it. No shot glasses. No decorum.

Then the longhaired one swipes it from her.

That is my damn tequila. It is like 99-octane here. "Give that shit to me!" I say, stealing the bottle from them.

Short hair says, "Are you Mexican?"

"Yes! That's why it's mine."

Long hair grabs and runs away with the bottle. Short hair distracts me by squeezing my ass to not chase the bottle. Laughs come out of her. She does not give a shit. An Arabic song comes on and she starts blocking my movement by belly dancing. She is shaking her breasts. Her ass.

"Are you really Mexican?" she says with incredible Botoxed lips.

"No. I come from a tiny country called Kuwait. Have you heard of it?"

"No way!" she says slowly.

"Yes way!"

"Your mother must be a foreigner."

"Must she?"

"Is she?"

"No."

Bosphorus is still calm, examining the entire charade. She is taking her own notes to use in the future for some sort of advantage. It is clearly written on that damn smug face.

Long hair comes back with a tenth of the bottle. "Listen, we're going to a party in Messila. It's a couples party. A swingers party. Wanna come?"

Bosphorus hears her, grabs my arm, and decides to shut off the Black Sea and the Sea of Marmara, "He isn't going anywhere! Istanbul is his destination tonight."

———

A minibus is wailing down the street blowing a wave of dust behind. Other cars are honking at it in anger. Drawing closer, it slams the brakes and the door opens. All the windows are either tinted very dark or curtained. The front windshield is tinted a third from the top. I can not see the bus driver or passengers.

"Geat in!" I hear an orchestra of Tagalog-sounding voices screaming.

I peer slightly in and see Skin laughing. He is driving the bus.

"Come up here and sit next to me."

"What the hell is going on?"

"I'm dropping off these fine people."

"Where?" I look back and some are all smirking and laughing. The others are gazing at their phones.

"Their work."

"What the hell is going on here? Did you steal this bus?"

"Habibi, it was borrowed." He then takes a sharp turn near a mosque and almost scrapes three or four cars. Few cars ahead are nervously looking in their rearview mirrors and honking out of fear.

Yes, ahead.

"Nothing is ever stolen," he says. "Things are only borrowed."

"Camelshit!" I tell him. "How'd you manage to get a minibus?"

"You wanted a lift, didn't ya?"

Skin changes into the fast lane on the freeway and draws close, way too close to a huge SUV, with a Kuwaiti man dressed in a freshly dry-cleaned headdress and dishdasha, intimidating and throwing pesty high lights at him.

He yells, "Get the hell off the lane, prick!"

Suddenly, the back of the bus all yell out in perfect Tagalog, "Chag 'is ass, sur."

I turn to Skin, "Did they just say, 'Shag his ass, sir?'" I turn back again, seeing some smirking and laughing while the others are sedated by their phones. "How do you know these people?"

"Company employees. Company bus. It's the only thing I could *borrow* to give you a ride."

"I didn't expect a damn bus!"

"Shut it, you should be so lucky. Better than paying a taxi driver who uses broken Arabic and English with loads of B.O."

"But a stolen bus with Filipinos is the answer?" squealing back.

"They are fine, hardworking employees. Now, SHUT it and open the glove compartment."

"Vapes?"

"No, habibi, papers. Get me those papers. All of them."

I hand him a stack of pink, blue and white company papers, and he flings them all out of his window.

"What the hell was that for?"

"Crap of crap. Of more crap," he says. "I'm being a conscientious patron of the arts and recycling like a good Kuwaiti citizen."

The papers land on different windshields behind us which causes heaps of honks.

More honks from cars in front are still coming out, though.

He sees my face is about to lose it, "Defensively offensive is the safest way to drive in Queerate," he says indicating the ambiguous sexual nature of most people here. "The best way to deal with queers here is to queer their sense of everyday living."

With tinted and curtained windows, and violent street action, so much that is hidden is shown openly.

We finally pull into a large parking lot with casual American diners in every corner. Skin screeches the bus to a halt in the middle of the street, not caring to park in any lanes. The employees—mostly women and gender-bending feminine males—all assemble out in their restaurant uniforms. Cars packed with families behind us honk-in noise pollution. Few of the women workers, and the women lookalikes, softly wave at skin saying, "Byyee suurr."

He finally speeds off, braking softly to the honking behind us to force them to drive around. Then Skin slams the brakes again making the bus quiver. It feels like it is about to completely break down, barely holding on to any sanity.

"See those cocks and balls?" he points to the most famous landmark in Kuwait.

"Kuwait Towers?"

"Yes, cocks and balls," he throws out while more cars have jammed up behind us. They are honking, throwing Kuwaiti slurs about bagging mothers and defacing parts of our sexuality, and finally throwing plastic cups at the bus.

"Those cocks and balls are imports. Look at them!"

The shapes do look like a set of penises and testicles.

"Swedes designed them because us citizens aren't allowed to design and build anything worthy in our own country," he throws his middle finger out the window to the honking. Most in the cars look like expats. "We're given full scholarships to study in their countries but can't build anything of worth back home. Now, we have cocks and balls laughing at us."

He finally speeds off. Two cars with young punks drive on both sides of the bus trying to threaten us. Skin opens his window a tad and slides out the tip of a toy gun. The punks decelerate. Quickly vanish.

We are in the slums of Kuwait City, the back roads where most of the unskilled male laborers reside. Minibuses, half lorries and taxis infest the tiny parking lot. Some of them are parked off the curbs, some half parked and some others fully parked on them. Skin leads to a restaurant where there is black residue on the outside walls. There are TV wires hanging outside, heavy cracks across the walls, water dripping from no distinct source.

Inside, we sit amongst the laborers. The waiter comes and asks what we want.

"Habibi, get this sorry-ass-of-a-man the best kebab you have," he says to the Persian-looking waiter. Skin lays out a black credit card to the edge of the scratched up table.

"Soltani Kebab?" the waiter asks.

"Yeah. Throw lots of butter on there, too."

"With buttermilk to drink?"

"Yes, habibi."

The waiter peers at the black card and says "Inshallah!" heading quickly to a half-lit kitchen.

"You trust this place?" looking around. All men. They all look exhausted. They all look beaten. "Will I be getting diarrhea soon after?"

"That won't happen. Trust these people, habibi. They are the guts of this country. When you learn to live with instead of against them, then you'll know their dedication."

"Like those Filipinos on the bus? And what's dedication have to do with food cooked properly?"

"Filipinos are incredible beings. So nice. So humble."

Pushing back at his hollow pitch, "So deceptively nice."

"Shut it! I work with them. Not against them. We help each other against the real thieves who run our company. Those nice people cover for me when I want a break from the madness. How else do you think I pick you up? They also give me homemade booze. The women in accounting hook me up with free business class tickets. They are lovely people."

"You corrupt son of a bitch."

"Shut it! That's mom you're talking about. How else do

you expect corruption in this country to be handled? Corruption breeds corruption, habibi. It's Kuwaiti Finance 101."

After we finish the heavy meal, the waiter comes back and says that the credit card does not work. It is null and void. He even has the balls to cut the card right in front of us.

I am not surprised.

How many times has Skin pulled the same scam on me all around the world when we travelled together? In Jamaica during a college spring break he ate a lavish breakfast right in front me, sipped leisurely on their Blue Mountain coffee, and then the waiter said his debit and credit cards were both emptied, after his stomach was stocked.

When we were heading back to Kuwait during Christmas break, we stopped in Chicago for a few days, and lo and behold, as we checked out, his cards failed. In Amsterdam, he had the gonads—yes gonads—to look at me peacefully while the receptionist declined his cards. And of course, there are way too many stories to remember in Kuwait.

The meal—Skin's usual antics—puts me in a laughing coma, so much so that I do not care anymore. I pay for everything.

"Nothing's for free, habibi."

"You'd know with all those whores."

"You don't think you pay?"

"Not for women."

"Habibi, you ALWAYS pay. The vagina is man's ultimate weakness. We have to date women, lie to them, and hear their crap just so we can get into their wetness. It's the worst kind of taxes. Taxing man's natural urge to release his tight valves for a short, few minutes."

"Get married then."

"So I can be assassinated by state, federal and happiness tax?"

We are back on the road. It is bitch hot outside, temperatures swelling into the 110s. I laugh it all off. Skin is one incredible scam artist.

He should be a haras.

Seeing me almost fall asleep in the bus, he says, "I'm heading to Thailand for a few weeks. Care to fund Skin's Amnesty Fund?"

"What?" He loves to use the third person singular when funds are involved.

"Have any funds to help out your younger brother? Every fils will go a long way. They'll go to very, very good use."

Fils are the denominations of the Kuwaiti dinar.

"You mean, help fund Skin the creditless fraudster live lavishly like a king?"

He laughs.

"How can an ex banker not know how to handle money? How can Skin never have cash? Worst of all, I've never heard of a banker not getting credit."

'When one has gone through war, lives amongst corruption, one's gotta hustle, habibi."

He stops at a bus stop and picks up an international group of manual laborers. "Fain rayheen?" his Arabic comes out in an Egyptian dialect to two labor-whipped men. Then he asks, "Saan ka pupunta?" to a Filipina. I assume it means where is she going.

"What the hell's going on?"

"Got to make gas money," he says.

Every few miles, he stops on the highway to let a few out. And take a few in. He tells me to go collect half a dinar from each person. One of the Egyptians sitting in the very back pulls out and starts smoking gido, a hard version of shisha without foil to filter the charcoal. There is just some hard tobacco and charcoal burning it through. He coughs a little after each smoke. But a smile stretches across his face.

Alhamdulillah.

This man has found happiness.

Does anyone give a shit here? Does anything make sense here? Sleep is taking me over, especially after a heavy meal. Especially after sweeter hustling. Is this a dream?

"Get out."

"What?"

"Get the fuck out!" yells Skin, rudely waking me from a mini slumber.

"Am I home already?"

"Yeah. I gotta go back to punch in."

No one is left in the back.

"All this maneuvering, back and forth in the mornings and afternoons, just so you avoid work?"

"The only way to stay sane in this insanity!"

He peels out the bus, causing much traffic congestion and honking.

———

Just downloaded a whole season of Narcos Mexico. Illegally. But in Kuwait, the illegal is the norm. The mass corruption the standard. The wallahis and inshallahs are the numbing friendly gestures. The show reveals the hilarious double-dealing that is the culture in Mexico. Fighting only accelerates it.

Sounds like Kuwait.

Suddenly, my building starts to shake. Shit! It is another

earthquake. The same happened exactly one year earlier at the same place on the Iraqi-Iranian border. That was a 7-point-something quake. This feels similar.

I put on some jeans, throw on a sweatshirt, immediately pack my backpack with an envelope filled with my passport, birth certificate and other important papers, and throw in American dollars, British Pounds and Euros. Oh yeah, wallet, glasses and sunglasses are arranged in their proper compartments, too.

Down the stairs I jog. Outside are groups of Central Asian workers in the open parking lot. Most of them bunk in groups of 4 to 6 in the building in the same style apartment as I have.

Government regulations, my ass.

All these people are trying to move away from any ruble that may come down. A few cars are speeding out of the parking spaces in the basement.

The quakes and the latest chemtrail spraying in the skies that produce heavy rain and flooding are geoengineered. Either they are hiding Nibiru, or war with Iran is coming.

Or both.

The Rothschilds need to boost the fake worth of the dollar after Russia and China have recently moved away from it.

The Haras crosses the street and chuckles, "Nothing's going to happen, ya Basha."

I have had it so much with this country that I am just numb to anymore spectacle. "I assume you are an expert in quakes to say something like that?"

"Wallahi . . ."

Once that comes out, I cross the street back against a herd of people coming down, take the elevator up to my demoralizing apartment and continue to watch an illegal episode of Narcos.

Earthquake or no earthquake, I have had it!

My phone gets a message, "Hey asshole," from another unknown number. I message back, "33?" I quickly check the country code and it is from Nigeria.

"You in Africa? In Nigeria?"

She immediately types back, "I'm hot and bothered. When are you going to put a stop to my juices? 33 requires taming."

Damn the use of the third person singular to address oneself!

33 loves to tease. She has me addicted. Has me fixed. Strung. Why can I not block this woman from my life?

"How? Are u in the country?" I type back.

"Don't think too much. You'll lose sexual credibility," she messages right back.

Where in the hell is this woman? Why does she always seem to hover like a ghost?

I hear a light knock on the door. No one knocks on my door like that besides 33. Looking through the peephole, I see her outrageously alluring white skin. Pink hair is this week's theme, though. I open up, "I thought I told you to never come unannounced."

"Grandpa, please." She pushes through, flings her shoes high in the air, throws her bag across the floor, and hugs me into her soft bosom. She hugs lightly, breathing her 33 years of streaming heat into my neck, grabbing and firming my tush. I shut up very fast.

"Who followed you this time?" I try to ask.

"A young imbecile in his 20's." Still, luscious breaths are sunk into my neck.

We are still hugging, but I can feel she is glaring into her phone behind my back. One finger is gently straightening her hair down, like a Millennial posing for thousands of fake followers on social media. I attempt faintly, "He followed you all the way here?"

"You know it!" she says to tease me into jealousy. "He blocked my car from the back and tried talking to me."

"And?"

"I blew him off. Why would I need a young turd who'll finish in 30 seconds when I have a matured asshole who will last 30 minutes?"

She pushes me away with the right hand that is not using the phone. Then she slaps my face with it. "Now go into the bedroom. Ms. Morpheme needs to teach the wannabe writer a lesson or two about linguistic appropriation after I use the ladies' room."

The Haus invites me to a dinner party in the richest area in Kuwait adjacent to Kuwait City, Thahia Abdullah Salem. When the parallel stock market called the manakh inflated and corrupted egos back in the 70's and 80's, many profited and bought and established homes in this area. The land of the super-corrupt is what it should be called. Many of the families living in the area have helped to direct economic policy to this day.

Again, The Haus wants to meet at her place. Downstairs, she makes me message and wait again. This time though, she comes down insisting that we go together in one car. Hers.

Shit! Whenever a woman wants to lead into a party, going their in her car, and having her drive too, I should expect to be controlled. Limited.

In her slick Range Rover, she drives in and out and between cars like a young male would, sharply cutting off young men who are cruising on Love Street searching to flirt with young women and transgenders. She is playing and raising the volume to a Kuwaiti rap song, which is in half Arabic and English badliyat.

Badilyat is a language of the Kuwaiti youth. In it is mostly pidginized Kuwaiti Arabic with English. Buffer zone is what is it. It defies classical modern Arabic by using heavy Kuwaiti, and it ushers in many American idioms. Together it comes out as a decoded language against older generations.

The singing duo are Bahraini-Kuwaiti, rapping and popping phrases about food and the typical nonsensical issues many face in Kuwait, as if the words mashed together are some sort of twilight zone. As if the Gulf region is a hot mess.

It is.

The eccentrically suave, belly-dancing Haus takes detours that get us lost further. She just laughs into the song. Into my face whenever she is driving so carelessly smoothly over speed bumps, continuously in circles around roundabouts, and speedily through U-turns. She is residually touring, belly dancing me into fear and excitement in one.

At the party, we are greeted by an older married couple.

"What's your name," the hosts ask.

"Nobody, with a capital N," I reply.

Inside, the first thing I spot is an organized bar. The typical whiskeys and other hard liquors in red and black colors await consumption against a mirrored wall; the alcoholic poison waits to open up humans into spelling out their innermost honesty.

I am offered one—quickly.

The Haus has her Russian assassin, as she should because that is how I see her: an assassin in many more ways than one.

There are mostly men who seem to be entouraging a married couple, the hosts' friends. One man is playing oud, the Arabic lute, and he is wearing a dishdasha, with the headdress curtained qitra flapped above his head, like most men do when there is physical work to be done. Two other men on each side of him are clapping hard, smacking their hands in a traditionally heavy percussive thwacking; giving rise to the singer who is playing the oud. A fourth man is beating on a clay jug as a bass percussion. One of them gets up and starts shuffling his feet, dancing one foot on his toes while the other foot drags behind. He shrugs his shoulders in perfect rhythmic sync with the jugging percussions, thumping down and pulling up his body.

The vocalist is laying out old poetic words of wisdom, melodious talk of being in mud-streeted homes amongst hardworking but gossipy neighbors and seafaring adventures on dhows to and from India and east Africa, where some of the musicians look like they originate from. The lead vocalist creaks and pulls back, spits out and catches the other musicians in a rhythmic trance. Their necks bounce up and down, bobbing from side to side, and clapping harder to the musical phrases popping out. The result is an echo of worded wisdom throughout the house's concrete walls; the echoes come and go, go and come as if they are straining—crying, as if they are recalling days gone past, when people's worth were measured in their simple daily lives. In their simple daily struggles.

The hostess motions that dinner is ready. Almost all of the food is Arabic, some specifically Kuwaiti. Machbous is the main dish. It sits smack in the middle of the table like a mountain. This machbous is made up of rice, fried lamb and then steamed for hours with various spices and daqous—a tomato based salsa with garlicky spices. It is damn delicious.

The hostess did a superb job with the food.

And music.

I go to the bar to talk a little with The Haus. She is laughing at the bartender's joke in French. Damn, she speaks Arabic, English, and French. Not bad for a young Moroccan woman who came out of a rural town to be thrusted into fame in Beirut's talent show called Star Academy when she was only an innocent 18, when she broke taboo because she did not wear a veil. According to her, that is where she learned to be a haus, a multifaceted entertainer. Visionary. Lover.

"Love is pure," she says with that mischievous smirk that is so hard to decode. I rarely know when she is laughing at someone or with them. There is a fresh Russian assassin in her hand. The woman can handle her booze.

She starts talking about Islam. She says that she does not believe in how man has corrupted the Quran with man-made Hadiths over the ages. "Their interpretations have ruined the purity of the Quran. It's men's Hadiths that have twisted Islam after Prophet Mohammed." She takes a sip. "The Prophet was pure. He was love."

In between sipping her assassin and romanticizing her version of Islam, she smiles at the other guests, never losing her composure. She works the room like a true professional.

Then she turns back to me, "Love is balance."

She smokes a very slim cigarette, a very womanish cig that is perfectly wrapped and tightened, yet the cigarette has so much density in pulling out a smoker. There is no pattern to her smoking. There is no addiction. Even the Russian assassin is somehow unpatterned.

Drinking it is one thing.

Finishing it is another.

Finishing her is completely another. What I see more clearly is how she controls both substances, juggling them according to the love she injects them with, personifying the cigarette and drink into lovers. Personifying temptation into love.

Playing them both.

Is this why?

Playing is her love. The entire process is love. With finesse and grace, The Haus commands her environment with precision, with great and fluid emotion. She is in love with the idea of love, the romantic notion of breaking down manmade processes and regulations. It is in the area that is unknown, the area that is free that she can become love.

In the twilight zone, she is an untethered master.

A woman comes up and hands her a microphone. She gently excuses herself and goes to the center of the living room, where the old Kuwaiti music has been playing. Sitting on the edge of a sofa, with legs carefully crossed and sensually black dress leading in eyes, she starts to sing. Softness streams through her vocal chords, pouring out through to her lips.

Words and feelings of love caught in a wrong time, because of a wrong control, play to people's truths. Everyone listening and watching is hypnotized. The audience and her are both feeding off each other. Without the other, both would cease.

The slave and master motif.

Then she stands up. Gutsy and elusive, The Haus drowns the men with her curvy hips. The women look at their men and blush. She is pulling the strings and enjoying it to death, causing panic and, without doubt, questioning when the couples go home.

One man who is soft on the eyes, and who has been staring at her all night, has the balls to approach and flirt with her using a typical sexual and Arab innuendo. The Haus just laughs him away by turning her face to one side between her singing. She demeans men who over stare or approach her with shallow hit ons. Charisma and carefreeness turn her on, igniting something wilder yet tamer. Rejecting such men is easy for her; she does it through fear, manhandling and scaring them, as if she is the man confidently hitting on an impressionable woman.

Consistent pursuit in a very original approach turns her on like a naked fruit, not the layered fruit that needs peeling.

The instrumentalists hit a snag or two without the right tunes. They eventually adjust. The Haus then sings her best to the audience, who have pinned their hopes in hearing her recite popular Kuwaiti Arabic tunes.

It does not seem to faze her. There seems to always be a smile resting across her face.

Every time she heightens a habibi or hoob, words of adoration webbed in love, The Haus swamps her audience into letting go of their inhibitions to emotionalize to a greater and more approximate need.

She is a high priestess and her followers are blindly abiding to her musical oration.

The party soon comes to a close. Driving back home through Love Street, The Haus deliberately plays with many young men chasing her in their flashy cars. In and out and between, she is tipsy, but somehow she controls the car with incredible flexibility, controlling her followers, controlling her environment, even if she is in a drunken mess.

So much control, yet so little sobriety.

Curious.

She turns down the music blaring about resisting forced love. "Do you know what I remember so clearly about my mother?"

"What?"

"Her faith." The Haus puts down one of two mobiles she is thumbing on the center console. "My mother was love," she says as if singing a love ballad. "My mother was balance," continuing while weaving the car throughout other souls, who may be lured by the flesh than the spirit.

I realize then that she is a woman who has been thrown into the limelight at an innocent young age as a pawn to sing and perform for other people's cursory leisure. An inanimate tool to fix animate, self-created issues.

Yet, she seems to hold on to the religious faith her upbringing—her mother—instilled in her. Her mother is faith to her, just like Allah is love to her. Just like Prophet Mohammed.

This woman's confidence marches forward in stride. This is a woman who emotionalizes everything confidently yet breaks taboo, an Arab woman who would be veiled if typical Arab men could control her. Married twice and divorced, her faith for life, for herself carries on like a religion.

"I remember my mother's love," she breathes out. "My mom's religious strictness while bringing me up was love." She turns off both phones. Turns off the music. "I only now understand why she was so tough. 'Be careful with men who come to steal your sex,' she used to say," looking straight ahead. "She used to advise me to become like men to play them."

The Haus describes how she had to not only survive but to crush men who usually came to Morocco as sex tourists, stealing the purity of young virginal women for a very, very limited pleasurable time; a limited pleasurable fetish.

Because of the awakening, she has attempted to give herself glory, playing the men who think they are players. As a result, it is the men who are left lingering. It is the men who are left searching for a faith they can not put their fingers on.

"Love isn't related to his penis," she says. "It's the kiss, the French kiss. That's love. There is a lot of sensitivity in the kiss. Love is a process, not an action. When I say I love you, it's not the end. It's the beginning. The journey."

She appears to be a queen, a player of hearts, yet love seems to be elusive to her. It is elusive to most people. She is always striving to reach it yet may not know how to handle it if she were to ever get it.

The idea of love does that for her. She loves detachment, too. The woman loves space, in love with the fringe of freedom. Singing is love to her. Territorial love is another. She will sacrifice and endure so much deception like cheating because of territorial love. Her loves are emotional and sexual intelligence. She protects her loves like a house (triangle): an Infiniti insignia. The infinity symbol stands for a number greater than any assignable quantity or countable number.

Love is giving, sharing without expectations in turn, like her mother's. Love frees her, like her mother's who has been a woman of context. Wearing a scarf on her head has not only been to submit to Islam, but it has been used as protection from more complicated women.

And, undoubtedly, it has been used against men who are simpler, especially in bed.

All this has opened The Haus's eyes to the culture of competition between women mixed with her mother pushing her siblings higher; sacrificing her own historical makeup as a precise and faithful Muslim mother to energize her children to become stand-alone powerhouses.

I do not think any man can tame The Haus, for her worth, her performances in various fields is her love. No wonder so many men want her. They love her purity, yet she is sexy. Men love her contradiction because it is unconquerable. She is unquenchable.

The lure is in the unknown.

They are lured by her dynamic and well-rounded character. They are lured by her continuously changing mysticism.

I am in love with just watching her perform. The control in her curves, voice, and eyes are prompts to her eventual dance of love. In her twists and turns of seduction and performance, she is balanced. Grounded. Validated.

Watching women like her, I get a deeper a sense of how women are mutable, changing with what comes along that validates their energies, moving with whomever can foster their interests. Borders and nationalities do not concern them as much as fluidity. Security. That is perhaps why they can marry and have offspring with men of other nationalities. They can become other citizens that are based on man's nationalistic descriptions of culture and identity.

Adaptability for women similar to The Haus gives them a liquid sense of identity. One that feeds into what they perceive as their own womanly makings. Their desires, their ideals come through and into a world that is unlike men's.

No wonder women network so calmly amongst themselves, without violent competition, as men often undergo. What would happen if women were in control of this planet? How would this world be different? Softer? Kinder? More nurturing?

Wait, are they not already in control from behind the scenes?

Women are shifty. Touristy. They are residual like the belly dancing, curvy and hypnotic Arabic music entrancing spirits. Their skin and muscle maneuvers dance to rhythms that invite a soul to exist for and in the moment, to eventually exit the soul to another way of life, so it could create a new but temporary culture to absorb.

DUBAI

Driving alone again, I start to mimic another accent. I am driving on the slowest lane on Feheheel Expressway heading downtown. This time the mimicry is of a Sicilian American. Deep and heavy, I bring out the street side of two male accents simmering toward a confrontation. Movie-style.

"Get the fuck outta heer. You hear me, Tony."

"You talkin' to me, Vincenzo?"

"Yeah, I'm talkin' toya. I said, getthe fucka ata heer."

"Get thefookatahee? Is that whatcha tellin' me?" I pack my right hand at my crotch and say, "I gottit right heer foryea."

I eventually turn off the charade and turn on the radio, allowing something else to entertain.

"For the many individuals who try to re-contact an old flame," the expert says on the radio program, "a boyfriend or girlfriend, let's say, from their high school or college days, may find themselves in a self-perpetuated trap."

"Self-perpetuated trap?" the male presenter asks.

"Yes. Out of five hundred individuals in my recent study who use Facebook, eighty-five percent of them have tried to reconnect with an old lover and restart a relationship for one reason or another, usually ruining their relationships or marriages in the process," she says while the radio host's voice stutters a little. The doctor of sociology concludes, "eighty-five percent fail in trying to reignite an old flame, resulting in going back to very little to nothing because of a past temptation rearing up its head in the present."

I increase the volume as the program is ending.

The female professional reiterates, "85 percent!"

———

River Thames.

7:28:35 PM: Messages you send to this chat and calls are now secured with end-to-end encryption.

"Hey wiseass," I type into the chat.

A message from her comes. "That is my middle name. I am glad you appreciate it."

There is no picture. There is very little history to analyze why she may have tried to reconnect after two and a half decades. I accept the message on FaceCrap.

Yes, Crap.

I do not understand why so many people spend so much time on this social media site revealing their intimate—insignificant—details to people they barely have ever known. So many personal photos show happy smiles, happy lives, happy lies.

Happy sappy happy.

Why must they be publicized to the world? Whatever happened to privacy? Personal space? The one profiting from this, and getting the last laugh, is the mediator: FaceCrap. It is collecting so much personal information by having individuals willingly disclose heaps without doing much in return. I am sure many of the valuable details go to agencies that would rather spy on people than directly engage them.

Do people waste so much of their lives on FaceCrap because of recognition? Acknowledgement? Loneliness? Pick your mess. It is probably one of them, if not all.

Plus some.

Everyone is a mess. Everything is becoming a mess. Is it aging? Am I unraveling? Shit, are traces of senility creeping up on me?

She is asking questions concerning health, work, and other shallow crap. I am sure she is testing my responses to see how I would want to engage her once again after dating her at 16. Why would she respond to a ghost message I sent years ago? Why now? Why so late?

I need to know.

"It takes one to truly appreciate another's wiseassing craft." I volley.

She finally breaks the chess maneuvering, "You are not a typical Kuwaiti, are you?"

"You should have received an answer to that when we knew each other as teens. Without any inkling of any doubt."

"Yeah, how come you are so different?"

"Raised always on the move. Kuwait, the UK, the US, so many other places in between. I have been buried in so many people, in so many cultures," I throw at her. "Tons of fancy but delicious trouble."

"If you do say so." She immediately chucks another shifty message, "Is that why your marriage ended?" And another, "Sorry—too personal. I take that back."

I am rereading the messages carefully, wondering why she would be so direct, wondering more about her beautiful bluntness.

"No. Marriage is not for everyone. After having

children, women—mothers change, we men are not needed," I feed her. I feed myself. This notion is killing, torturing yet freeing me. It is a wonderful paradox. I answer her one more attempt at philosophizing my recent mess. "We become immarital, stateless in marriage."

I just made that word up. Immarital.

"What ended yours?"

"Lies and my husband's inability to reconcile his previous life with ours. He was married before. Plus he drinks too much. But mainly his lies and his deep self-loathing."

Here goes another woman typically ranting about a failed relationship, most likely her own failed trials at changing a man according to what she fancies as just and truthful.

"Monogamy and compromise are killers of individuality," I type in. "They manifest the best lies."

I change the topic and ask if she has any pictures of herself? I am deeply curious to know what she looks like after decades, how people and circumstance have aged her.

"Ah you want to see if I got ugly in my old age?" She types in after a few minutes.

"I want to see HOW you aged." I repel back immediately to quash her doubts and to lure her through my way of thinking, to direct the chat.

"You will have noticed I have no photos on Facebook or here. Yes ok I will send some recent ones if I can rustle them up—bear with me. I haven't seen you since I was 15. I still remember everything."

Does she not mean 16? I am quite sure it was 16.

"Yes. Since I was your first, correct? I remember so many things with you too. Much chaos was created in getting to know you. I lost many supposed 'friends.' That's why I pursued you on FB, looking for any remnants of you. I envisioned you in the UK, with your sarcastic flare, stomping on imbeciles and the like, making hordes of them fall for your captivating mysticism: beauty."

"You will have to give me a few minutes to digest what you just wrote. Here are some pics to amuse you in the meantime."

No heavy eyeliner surrounds her eyes in the photos, like she used to wear in her teen years, where it brought out her mysticism to the world to try to play with. There is also no puffed out hair. It is flat, leaning over her facial cheeks. Barely any wrinkles on her face. It is clear, as cleanly alluring as it used to be in her youth. "You look good for a woman in her 40's."

Then I see a photo with a much older man with her. Too many years in difference. I tell her, "Wow, Thames! Why?"

"Why what? We did have some good times. I have only just grown up," she says about the man in the photo standing in front of her in what appears to be some European city. She is hiding her body slightly behind his. It is as if she is hiding, period. Is she hiding from life? Self-created disgrace? "You could have had so many men. Why so much older?"

"Needed me a father figure."

"Pity! Why no kids?"

"I never wanted kids. Am very happy as I am."

"I won't philosophize THAT to death just yet. Happy is an abstract word."

"I mean thank fuck I don't have any brats bringing me down," clinging on to self-reflective doubt, procreation.

I detour the topic, "Kuwait is a spiritual trap to stay all year in for me."

"You haven't changed much. Finally, I can see your eyes."

"Do you live alone?"

"Not yet but soon. I bought my own place and am waiting to move out. Till then am in the place my husband and I bought. We get on ok. I like Dubai. So you ever come here?"

"It's been a while."

"You should come. I will invite you to lunch. Do you drink wine or are you a strict Muslim?"

"How can I pass up a lunch? Wine was a fad in the 90's."

"Wine—a fad? That is a good one. You can share a bottle of good red wine with me and put the world to rights."

She seems to be tipsy right now. Alcohol, no matter what type or dosage, only temporarily numbs. Only momentarily hides.

"Righting the world with you would be a much nourishing, and balanced, experience. Dubai is so materialistic, isn't it . . ."

———

It was at a party during my senior year in high school that I clearly remember grabbing a chunk into her primal teen years. Me and my international school friends from the likes of Sweden, US, Indonesia, and of course Kuwait, were partying at a Kuwaiti's house we did not know, as was the norm. Most of the guys in the circle started having relationships with girls from NES—New English School. They were little teases. The young seductresses also composed their own international crowd, ranging from hybrids as Kuwaiti-Scot, Palestinian-Swede, a Fijian-Spaniard, Iraqi-Austrian, and of course Palestinian-Austrian. That Palestinian-European, though, would haunt me for years.

River Thames.

Thames was dating the Swede from our crowd during that party in early October. I saw her pulling three guys from my school by hypnotizing them with her erotic red, flashy lipstick, indicative of 80's panache. Hair wavy, Thames would flip it from one side to another every few seconds, having one streak snake down her face to induce the young men into a sexual frenzy. Abused it well she did. And she spoke with a stiff English accent. She spoke with her face, not her mouth. It was too controlled, too disciplined. Too much composure usually calls for—yearns for—breakage.

British accents have always sounded strange on Arabs, especially from an Arab who was brought up with an American accent such as myself. British accents sound weak, like they have not had enough extra curricular activities, especially varied sports, like they need to be rescued from their own disciplined suffocation.

Dating was the furthest I went. Fuck relationships. Fuck monogamy. It did not work then. It has not worked ever since.

I studied her for a few minutes before going in for the kill. I approached them and heard her talking about some insignificant thing or another. Drawing closer, I listened quietly to what she had to say.

The guys were talking about the River Thames in American accents, which the "Thames" bit is pronounced like the word "tames" but with an "h" after the "t." To Brits, however, it is pronounced "Tims." She started correcting the guys' American, what she called deformed vernacular accent, with the correct pronunciation.

Then and there I decided to call her River Thames, not only for her poise and manner with which she protected and projected the original English language but symbolically because of the river's stretched out length and fame in southern England, most notably going through London, through so many individuals and their daily lives to influence their most inner sense of spiritual and perceptual geography.

It probably has influenced their parlance as well.

I listened to her body language much more than to any other words or phrases that came out. She was hot. Sizzling. I wanted to take her. I wanted to pave over her, like all the other girls during my high school years.

I interrupted her flow of words by drawing closer and asking her, right in front of the other young men, "Are you a good kisser?"

That was it. I did not say anything else.

She stopped because of my brazen inquiry. Thames paused her rigid river of Englishness because of my blatant fearlessness to push things to the limit, if not cross and redefine it. Her eyes tightened a little, but she cracked a smile.

She cracked all right.

That was precisely my motive, to make her break. To make her lose her composure. And, for her to acquiesce to the unknown. I wanted her to surrender to the unraveled.

I—myself—wanted to submit to the unsolved. I constantly want to submit to my constant change of self.

The River drew up close and said, "Let's find out, shall we?" using a tag question so indicative of a Brit, but she was also whispering seduction in my eyes and into my lips from a close, uncomfortably comfortable distance, pulling my wrist lightly toward an outside corridor of the villa toward a kitchen and maids' quarters. We found a tiny maid's room. Practically all families living in Kuwait then had maids' quarters, had a maid.

Practically all families in Kuwait now have a maid. Or

two. Very little has changed. Just more maids for an inflating population of spoiled brats.

We breathed heat into each other, kissing our sins into the other. Her lips were damn tender. I was right. They needed moisturizing. They required heat and soft mass to light up all the other parts of the body that were rigidly closed because of laboring, Muslim taboos, in a country that was trying hard to open up to the rest of the world culturally at the time.

What the hell was she doing with a Nordic? Are they not frigid? What she needed was spice. Arab spice. A spice that she was half born with. I gave her full spice, though. That kiss sealed what would come to be a spicy but unorthodox relationship for quite a few months during my senior year. It was a chaotic but welcoming mess.

Welcome to the Middle East. The whole region is a falafel of a mess. We are stuck in our own rut.

Most of the rest of my senior year was spent cheating on her, mostly right in front of her, wanting to get caught, wanting to be exposed and reprimanded for any attempt at monogamy.

Monogamy! What a lie. Why do people lie to themselves? It rarely works, and if it does, there are so many secrets that are built and pent up that it would make much more sense to release them for the sake of holding on to any sanity that may be left than to go crazy by deceiving the partner for longer periods of time. By deceiving oneself for much longer, traumatic, and incurable periods of time thereafter. MonogaLIE.

MonogaHELL.

A well-known Turkish coffee in Kuwait and Jordan jostles River Thames as she sips, suspiciously, the oily drink. As she conspicuously drinks at me. We are in a small organic café. The River is going to gladly show me this end of Dubai. It is called Jumeirah Lake Towers. She lives and works in the area.

This part of Dubai is popping rapidly. Shiny buildings stick out of the boiling desert and humid Arabian Gulf.

Sorry, Persian Gulf.

Expats work and live in most of these buildings. It is very organized. Most of the people I see look European, white. Anglo-Saxon.

Where are the brownies? Do they not own this country anymore?

She starts to journey me through her history, appetizing her gorgeous Palestinian heritage. She starts on a personal ride through her Palestinian dark brown eyes— culture. She starts to unveil the Arab identity she has had to mask with her European side.

"I've been escaping my father's heritage for so, so long," the Thames rivers out. "My father worked for Kuwait Oil Company. You knew that, right?" her eyes tightly flashing. "He worked there for so long," slowly landing the little Turkish cup on its saucer. "Many of my relatives helped Kuwait grow," she says with greater confidence but with a touch of cry.

I am quiet, listening to her weave in and out of her storytelling, in and out of her personality. I catch a few strong glimpses into her womanhood. She seems to be yearning for acceptance, a yearning for all that she has accomplished being half an Arab who is trapped as a European in a woman's body.

"My grandfather had come to Kuwait way before," lifting and sipping at the coffee again. "I was born there. I am from Kuwait," her voice escalating. "I *am* Kuwaiti!"

I continue to listen. But it is hard at times because her glossed lips tempt and divert from focusing on her words. Her voice is beginning to sound angry, squeaking and tremoring in intonation, like Kuwait has neglected her, like Kuwait has forgotten to appreciate her and her family for helping to develop it. Perhaps, she is trying to have me sense her as a woman and as an Arab and European for helping to cultivate Kuwait into a cosmopolitan state without forgetting its Arab heritage.

Just perhaps.

Perhaps, because I am a Kuwaiti citizen.

Kuwaiti citizenship can not be gotten by simple birth. It is usually passed down through paternal inheritance. Only very few are naturalized per year, ones that the government deems worthy for helping out the country according to critical vocations like medical doctors, high-end educators, engineers, and specially the women who marry Kuwaiti men. The women who dilute and stretch out the old Kuwaiti.

"Most of my family lived there," she stops my train of thought with a soft tremble in her voice. "I feel so damn attached to that place," slowing her tempo much more. "Kuwait *always* seems to call me back," she says like a poet reading a poem out loud.

"It's always calling me back," staring into the oil, the coffee. "Back home."

"Why haven't you visited it since liberation?" trying to learn why Kuwait has influenced her so much even though she has lived in other parts of the world.

She pauses a little, diving into the swampy, undrinkable remnants of the Turkish coffee and says, "I sense fear going back." She looks out through the café's large front window, "But something is drawing me back," whispering to herself. "I must go back. The desert is always calling me back."

Thames's father used to work at Kuwait Oil Company as a petroleum engineer who was brought in by the ruling family. They all lived in Ahmadi, a place further out and away from other parts of the country, a place where the Brits carved out a community to call home away from home. V-shaped roofed houses, left-sided driven streets, little performing arts theatres and recreational clubs, and heavy imported green vegetation made Ahmadi stand out amongst other areas in Kuwait. It was a little Britain.

It was not Kuwait, that is for sure. I remember the place being a sheltered European community smack in the middle of Arab, albeit awkward, dynamism. Some Brits used to call Ahmadi a sanctuary, a respite from the chaos and mayhem that was typically seen in multi-Arab-influenced Kuwait.

Different areas of Kuwait had and still have different feels. They have been little cosmopolitan models of greater Arab cultures right in the middle of one of the tiniest Arab countries.

No wonder Kuwaitis have always felt that they are a minority in their country! They have been. They are. Very little has changed since River Thames was last there.

Her birth and upbringing in mostly Kuwait's undeveloped desert back in the 70's spring out. She roasts them through storytelling as a few pistachios are crunched in between. "My family started the first-of-its-kind coffee in Kuwait," she casually lays out. "You know it, right? It's well known for its Turkish coffee."

"I do."

"It's this same coffee we are drinking now."

"Is it?"

"Well, it's not the same now. The Kuwaiti owner made

many changes to it. The coffee just doesn't taste the same like when my grandfather started it back in the 70's with the Kuwaiti partner."

"Kuwait's not the same now." I tell her. "Some things have gotten worse."

"How?"

"Lots of sprawling corruption. The government is weak, but it's trying to patch things up. If it ever succeeds, it will be after decades."

Cardamom crawls out of her coffee cup, dancing around my stubborn ego, dazzling my yearning for emotional stimulation. It is drenching my immediate senses, oozing out of her essence, spicing me with a love of nostalgia.

With a love of now.

We leave the café and take a break from some of her Kuwaiti past. I rarely understand why so many Arabs desperately want to be Kuwaiti, yet many Kuwaitis take their own citizenship for granted. Is it because of complacency? Surely.

Thank goodness I have never felt fully Kuwaiti, or any other nationality.

People like me are often part of many cultures yet not. We go through nationalities yet rarely depend on them to define us. We are cultural and personality warriors, moving and consuming culture along the way, but we do not want to settle anywhere, chiefly not nationalistically. Identity should not have borders; vague constructs that do not appeal to the beauty of being spiritual wanderlusts.

In spirit, I am my own nationality. I am my own patriot.

I see a large artificial lake. It is clean. Too clean. The sidewalks around it are pristine. There are not any gum stains whatsoever. There is not any littered trash on them of any kind. A darkie—a Southeast Asian—is cleaning any waste whities may have accidently left behind. He does not look into anyone's eyes. His eyes just sweep trash.

In Kuwait, such a cleaner is usually pot-bellied, looks into people's eyes for monetary sympathy. He often gets it from guilt-ridden and conscientious women because they are the easiest to fool.

Such deception is equally seen during shopping. Women fall prey to details, to colors and shiny things that are further sugarcoated with slippery words. With slippery lies.

Dubai's skyline is riddled with skyscrapers; shiny, glittery buildings barging into the sky, out of the brown and sandy desert and into a glassed house with a delicate, breakable ceiling. Structures that seem to defyingly climb, climb and continue to climb endlessly, with unnatural materials like high-end glass and steel, are not of the desert environment. And they stretch toward a natural sky, which does not seem to want to accept them. It is a mirage, all right. It is a Las Vegas sprawling city railing fast to a very potential 1984 society.

It is also like River Thames' Ahmadi. A mirage adopted from another culture to comfort foreigners—expats—into bearable living in a geography and terrain foreign and unnatural to them.

Jumeirah Lakes Towers looks utopian. Most of the menial workers constructing new office buildings and apartments are from India and other impoverished, rural areas of Asia. They are brought in like packed animals, stacked in buses and housed in faraway cities so that Dubai's rich and cosmopolitan image is not stained by the very people who are building, cleaning and servicing the place. They are unwanted refugees, slaves cast into a newly made caste to dehumanize them into serving a city built on materialism, rendered by foreign consumption.

And monitored and controlled by the minority of Emiratis, who are silent but watching. Who are a strong minority in their culture as it quickly dies to foreign invasion. Foreign capitalism. Foreign acculturation.

Orwellian is what it feels like.

They even have a Ministry of Happiness led by a self-described happy young woman to whip unpleasantness into shape. If you are not buying—consuming—then you are not happy. If you are not consuming—keeping busy—then you are abnormal. If you are abnormal, then you are deplorable. If you are deplorable, then you are deportable.

Up to eighty-eight percent of Dubai's residents are temporary workers. Foreigners. Any dissention would land a temporary worker in either jail, and this is no first world country type of jail, or expelled from the country. How in the hell would the Ministry of Happiness address that? By flying in and employing happy people that go along the rulers' stance?

Even citizens have had their citizenship revoked during a time when the UAE, alongside Kuwait, the rest of the GCC, Jordan, Morocco, Egypt, and Pakistan are expected to go along with Saudi Arabia's supposed coalition force, against its neighboring country of Yemen.

The Minister of Happiness is a Millennial. So is the Saudi leading the coalition.

Kuwait is doing the same. It is illegal according to Kuwait's constitution to go to war with another country that is not invading it, yet Kuwait is sending ground troops and even aerially bombing Yemen back into the Stone Age.

Yemen is already the poorest Arab country.

The Gulf is gearing up for something. Something much bigger than Yemen is coming. It will alter how the GCC sees itself and how it will be seen.

That is probably why there are no retirees from non-

Gulf countries in Dubai. Only citizens of Arabian Gulf countries like Oman, Saudi Arabia, Qatar, Bahrain and Kuwait are allowed to retire here without a business license. Only non-GCC expats who open a business can retire here.

A 1984 utopia!

White Europeans, Australians, North Americans, and Russians have come, brought their businesses here to what they think is a tax haven. Much of it is laundered.

However, the Emiratis have cunningly calculated and administered heightened fees through utilities, road tolls, and other unnecessary amenities to serve a lavish illusion—a mirage—to mostly an international vibrant youth. They are much more impressionable, controllable, and easily taxable.

The dark Asians are left behind. Forgotten in history as usual. Why? Because they were not brought up the same, did not have the same accessibility to education and other human necessities as many Anglos have had. Because their dark color also has been seen as dirty, echoing disease and hardship unless they have brought enough green money with them to help spread the city's image to the rest of the world.

"Whites are privileged here," she says while we are moving from one marina to another. Most marinas are located between mountains of buildings. The place is eerie, too quiet for so many man-made structures. For so many man-made facades built to amuse people's temporary appeasements.

It is too organized!

It is very unlike Kuwait. Thank goodness I am Kuwaiti where white expats may feel they are inferior. Kuwait is a mess, but Kuwaitis at least visibly run their country, albeit we are a minority in Kuwait, but a bigger minority than

Dubai's.

Dubai is imperial colonialism all over again. But this time, whites are allowed to live in a disillusioned utopia constructed and governed by an invisible force of brown, groups of tribal Arab mafias. Only a tiny handful of the richest and most influential families of Emiratis control an international horde, yet they are invisible—wizards of oz behind a materialistic curtain.

Oh yeah, Dubai also has a Ministry for Tolerance that not only seeks to tolerate the diverse peoples of Dubai, but it also wants to discipline the world, too.

Rich!

A phone number I do not recognize with an Irish country code calls. "Hello?"

"Hey asshole." I hear her intimidating but sensual laugh.

"33?"

"Where are you this time?" she asks softly.

"Afar."

"Some asshole at the supermarket wouldn't let it be. He had to follow me up and down aisles and to my car, eyeing me to death."

I move to a more private space. "Did you fuck him?"

"Asshole, please!"

"What do you want? I'm busy."

"Not busy enough to answer."

"Are you in Ireland?"

"Maybe."

"Get to the point."

"Service, asshole. I need to be SER-VISSED, bitch!"

"How? I'm not in the country. You don't seem to be either."

"Well, then I'll just have to ask a strange pair of goggle eyes."

"Bitch! Wallahi . . ."

She hangs up.

"Who was that?" Thames asks.

"A ghost. A nobody."

We walk over a bridge along a canal. Cafes and restaurants wait in every nook.

"What do you think?" River Thames asks. "Is it the same Dubai you remember?"

It is not. It is very futuristic. It is another Singapore. Hong Kong. "No, the place is different," I tell her.

"I truly like living here. There is so much to offer. So much to do," she lets out.

I remain quiet. Tourists are everywhere. Even the residents living here seem to be tourists.

Near a big boat dock that takes people out to sea, a brownie approaches and opens a glistening photo album of boats and food, trying to sell us tickets. He makes Thames fidget a little.

"Do I look like a tourist to you?" Thames says to him in her disciplinary English accent, escalating her voice. "Well, do I?" angrily throwing back at him.

"No madam. Sorry." He bows his head, moves back, abashed by her harsh reprisal.

I guess even residents who may think they are citizens feel the urge to mistreat each other.

She then says, "Residents know who the tourists are," and eyeing him in the process as we continue our trek around the marina.

"How?" I ask.

"It's clear," she says while staring at passersby. "We dress differently. We walk differently. We are quieter."

"Explain."

She points to a woman wearing a tank top and shorts yelling to her boyfriend or husband. "Like her," she says quietly. "Dubaiins dress more appropriately. We dress professionally. We talk more faintly."

That sounds like most Brits regardless of where they are in the world, especially when they are sober.

Moving along some more of one marina or another injected with shops and cafes, we stop at a bridge. The water is a clean bluish-green. I take a panoramic look around. I do not understand how so many buildings sit side by side, yet there is no echo from anywhere. It is so quiet. So eerily too silent.

"Do you know," she suddenly says while staring from the bridge and into the hypnotizing blue water, "what sort of impression you've left on me since I was 15?"

"Impression? Don't you mean 16?"

"15!"

"No. Tell me."

"You've been the only man to have such a long lasting impact on me in my womanhood."

Her face is so delicious to look at. What would it be like to kiss and skin-brush it again? She stares at me without blinking, without flinching, waiting for some sort of acknowledgment.

"But I only knew you for a few months. Are you telling me that I had a ripple effect on you, all because of a few months during your 16th year?"

"Paardon me," the stiff British accent comes out, "it was 15. And yes, you had a devastating effect on my adult life."

I just look at her, slightly cringing inside. Slightly cringing my facial cheeks. I do not remember influencing her that much.

"You've been the only man that has ever touched me the way you have."

I am bewildered. I am not sure if she is joking, but her death stare says she is not. Her eyes just x-ray, waiting for a slip.

Can it be? My words are interrupted by my surprise. I can not seem to say anything.

"Cat got your tongue?"

"It's got much more. I don't believe it. It just seems too unbelievable that I could have had any impact on your adult life. Why?"

"You were my first. No one ever came close to what I felt for you."

"You didn't show it," I tell her while her face is as numb, is as confrontational as I remember it. Poised, without any twitch, sitting there trying to expose any truthfulness, like a German S&M dominatrix would. "Why no one else? I am sure there have been much better men along the way!" I try to amuse myself in secret.

"No one! In fact, every boyfriend after you resembled you one way or another, yet they were never you. Never! I have always been attracted to men with your dark eyes, thick jet-black hair, and charm. Ohh . . ." she elongates with a little laughter, "it was your charm that's eluded me for so long."

I still do not answer. I do not have an answer.

"Fuckah!"

Our dialogue is interrupted by an East Asian manual laborer who brushes my back while riding a Royal Classic 28T Hero bicycle, the typical and popular classic bike commonly ridden by Indians. Made in India, ridden by them the world round. Kuwait included.

He turns around bobbing and weaving his head saying "soree" to mean "sorry," but at the same time, he stares at Thames' deep V-necked T-shirt, the shirt that shows too much skin, too much bosom, which is lots for the imagination of any man to handle, especially for men who work long treacherous hours amongst only men. It is just too much cleavage to hold himself in par with civilized manners. He loses his balance and falls off his bike.

Thames unleashes a cement but timid laughter.

I am just staring at the antics, the theatrics that I just imagined seeing the River Thames exquisitely produce, with that of the biker slightly hitting me, and the eventual crash, because of a woman's temptation. And her yearning for emotional balance, for emotional closure that never seems to come to a close.

We decide to keep walking so that she can show me the proper Dubai, through her eyes. After strolling through blocks of towering buildings, we arrive at one popular beach or another in Dubai Marina. Gorgeous Porsches, Range Rovers and Lamborghinis define the area. The cars are driven by mostly expats.

Wealth. There is so much of it. Or, there are so many attempts at attaining it. Thames asks if I mind having lunch at a Greek restaurant. I tell her no.

She eventually finds the Greek restaurant she has wanted to eat at for supposedly so long. It is located right in front of an open beach area. We sit down, and a non-Greek looking server comes. His English is heavy, rusty, as if his vowels are hard to pronounce. Thames does not know Arabic, so I ask him if he speaks it because there is too much English in Dubai.

Too much Englishness.

He says yes in a Moroccan Berber accent, where he uses a lot of the deep "ayin" (ع) sound. It almost looks like the Arabic numeral 4 (٤). It also looks like the inverted Om symbol (ॐ). The "ayin" is stressed in the back of the throat, as if phlegm has been accruing. "Jeem" is another letter he uses that is stressed but in the front of the tongue, where it reaches the lower lip about to be spit out but stops at the tip. The letters are similar to how Bedouins in Kuwait use them between themselves. He smiles and I order for us through his Arabic.

Moroccan is harsh.

So is Kuwaiti.

We both get by. We hold on to Arabism how ever slight it may be in our transaction. It is a proud sensation. However, I have to translate everything back in English to Tims.

There are many people on the promenade. Men and women, young and old, and children are walking along happily in their shuffle. A few are snapping selfies to probably post on one social media platform or another. FaceCrap would surely be one of them, especially for the older individuals.

I still do not get it! Unless! Unless social media is part of a sinister plan to socialize everyone under a new paradigm shift. Under socialism for the West while the East is moving towards capitalism and democracy.

Most of the selfies will probably go on Instagram, which is owned by FaceCrap, where everyone seems to be a hero, an instant celebrity because of how and what they post online. Most of the posts are rubbish, crap built on little to no talent. Both the app and most on there deserve each other's crap.

I guess the art of nothingness is the new trend.

I guess mindlessness is the new genius.

Two-piece bikinis, and other enticing swimsuits, catwalk along this promenade by mostly more Westerners. Healthy, childbearing bosoms, flat stomachs, highlighted hair, puffed dark sunglasses, and the occasional high heels walk along. Few Lebanese and Egyptian women in their tight-knit groups follow nearby with mostly their men body guarding them, preserving their own man's world so that women do not get too much freedom. So that they do not lose too much of their East, patriarchal control to an overwhelming Western invasion.

One tall Egyptian man is holding his woman to what seems to be his wife by the wrist, not her hand, and he is a step or two in front of her, not walking horizontally with her.

Symmetry is vital. So much so that it can define language when words are not used, what words can not define.

How do I know he is Egyptian? By his boisterous words and accent. It has to be stronger, more overpowering than his woman's, mainly in public. He would be a handful to physically deal with. I am sure he knows because of how he clearly demonstrates it, using body language with his female. Or, he like so many Arab men might be insecure about other men staring at his woman, about men perhaps stealing his woman from him. Arabs seem to always be paranoid about their own people, thanks to their own design. It is a self-created and self-entrenched mess.

A DJ is cooking lounge music comparable to Ibiza's libertarian atmosphere.

Am I in Spain?

A rare few women in tight black abayas suddenly show up along the walkway and ruin all that. They are flaunting portions of their inner—truer—personas. Henna-colored hands peep out to the public. Bottom seams of their Western jeans also come out to play with bright blue and orange sneakers. Kohl eyeliner is worn so typically, to ward off the evil eye, and to attract and trap the Arab men's sense of dominating control.

I see two young fit Caucasian women. They are attractive. One has very blonde hair, long legs, and blue eyes, wearing a ravishing bikini, covered by a light clothing sheath. A hard language comes out of her mouth. It sounds

Russian. Slavic. Somewhere in that area where women are dangerously gorgeous, calculative like assassins.

They *are* assassins.

They without any doubt know how to use their beauty to assassinate the men they think will assist them in climbing life's ladder to financial success. Why are women like these usually in Dubai? Even in the 90's and 2000's, lots of women from those regions were brought here for succinct purposes.

Prostitution. That is why.

They have been brought here for the oldest trade known to man. The sex trade. Who has brought them? Prostitutes are pimped by the same families who control Dubai, and they ship them in to de-stress most of the single men who have not been allowed to bring the rest of their family because of work probation and unqualified salary caps. Other than Western European and North American countries, the call girls are mostly planed in from Russia, Kazakhstan, Turkmenistan, Tajikistan, Uzbekistan, Kyrgyzstan; stans that most have barely heard of from Central Asia. Their visas, apartments, bodyguards, and other amenities are usually provided by the same sheikhs and top family mafias who preach Islamic virtue and decency to other Gulf Arabs and the rest of the world. Especially to their own citizens.

They control the import and export flow of the sex trade. Why would they not? Dubai does not have the same oil wealth as Kuwait does. It has to look elsewhere for prospects. Service is their top shelf industry. Serve and service the men with whores, serve and service the wives and children with retail, serve and service all of them with—exquisite but costly—comfort, and then everyone will be happy.

Thank goodness for the Ministry of Happiness!

And Tolerance!

"Fuckah!" River Thames flings ever so slowly, like her word is a drug being casually released. Like her profane use of this word is endearing, a word awakening something steadily in me.

"What?" I try to discover. "What did I do this time?"

"I saw you staring at those Russian women," eyeing with her sixteen year-old lip gloss, gorgeous eyes, eyeing with her flat lined, London accent. "What a shite you are!"

"Yes, I was and I'm still staring." I laugh at her, laughing more at her British usage of "shit."

She can not seem to hold her usual control and releases an uneven smile. A crack is appearing. "What? Are we in a relationship now?" trying to throw her off.

She just studies my words quietly. Thames just absorbs my revolt at being controlled by a woman. Her cheeks are slightly blushed. Her lips are not smiling anymore. Her eyes are squirming. She is in pain. We both made it clear before coming to Dubai that we were both disinterested in starting anything. Why? Because we are both coming out of divorce. It would make little to no sense to try to start any form of compromise—monogamy—when we both seek answers that only we can find by being alone.

"Did I hurt you?"

"No, of course not!" throwing her napkin on the table, thrusting back her seat, and softly excusing herself, "Just let me go to the LOO first," meaning to go to the ladies room, but before leaving, she says, "You're a nutter."

What just happened?

Women! That is what happened! They are peculiar creatures. They are not as direct as we men normally are. Tantrums are usual indicators that the opposite of what they say or do is the honest truth.

Is anything ever clear between the sexes?

So, she is jealous. Is that what it is? She must be. Fine. Let her be. I have come to visit her as someone of the past but yearning to hold on to only the now. Not the future.

While I wait for her, I stare at the beautifully alluring women all over the place. They humiliate women back home. Women in Kuwait need to catch up. They are way behind. Here, women show more natural skin. There, they show more synthetic skin—plastic surgery. Here, they are more naked, baring perhaps more of their personalities. There, they hide more with fuller makeups, masking internal personalities that may have never been educated to come out into the open and be an unprocessed human woman.

I can not blame them. I do not. I believe they are the makings of living under men's control. Under men's religion, and under men's perceptions of control. Kuwaiti women are repressed because of fear and shame.

Fear. Shame.

Many Arab women feel the same way. I sense it.

Many women the world over probably live under a similar mortifying humiliation.

The Tims comes back but with a more guarded poise. Sitting down mechanically and pulling her chair in civilly, she gets on her phone quietly, tapping on and raising her eyebrows every so often. She is most likely checking social media to get a distraction away from my supposed rude emotional behavior.

"Did you know that WhatsApp is blocked here?"

That is the only thing she says for a while. Since she does not want to talk to me directly, I too get online and look up any articles I can find about why the social media application would be blocked. I discover that applications that allow free phone calls like WhatsApp and Facebook's Messenger are both blocked. Could it be because both apps are owned by FaceCrap? No!

The reason is because authorities in Dubai want to eavesdrop on their residents and visitors, but FaceCrap will not comply even though they surely do it, too. BlackBerry had a similar problem with Dubai a few years earlier because they did not want to reroute or share their servers with the local government.

Reading related articles, I find that light displays of affection like kissing—never mind full-blown out sex—are censored in cinemas. OSN shows the same programming totally uncut, though. Yes, it is the same OSN satellite service owned by the Kuwaiti Emir's son. The same son who reportedly brought in a heavyweight Jewish billionaire investor to bloat and collapse the Kuwaiti stock market in the 2000's.

Inshallah, habibi!

I take a short break and look out to the water. Where in the hell are the average Emiratis? I only see a miniscule amount. They can probably be found in shopping zones similar to what Kuwaitis do. Shopping traps like Dubai's newest mall that steals more than heals souls.

"If you don't discuss politics, everything's fine," the Thames breaks the silence. "Just don't slander the Emir here and everything's grand. Just grand!" the River teases "grand" in an Irish accent that she says she has grown fond of and adopted from her Irish friend. "I mind my own business and no one bothers me."

A European-looking couple sits behind Thames. They order some fancy wine. It makes me promptly ask Thames about alcohol, because from what I remember back in the 2000's, authorities made it difficult for Muslims to purchase liquor from liquor stores. Buying it from restaurants and bars, though, was permitted. Pricy beers and hard liquors were tolerated.

Cash comes first before personhood here.

I am sure we can all thank the Ministry of Happiness for that!

And Tolerance!

She says that everyone must apply for a liquor license to the nearest police station to buy booze. If you are Muslim, it would make no sense to apply. They are not usually allowed to get a license because alcohol is forbidden in the Quran. Then there is an interview. All must go through an intense interview at a local police station to get an alcohol license.

How dandy! One has to be interrogated to get a license to an addiction!

———

Strolling under buildings and throughout car parks in Jumeirah Lake Towers, we are heading into an Irish pub located underground like a dive bar, in an Irish-owned hotel. Before getting there, we pass another of the hotel's bars.

"This is where all the African whores catch their prey," the Thames spews with a fidgety face.

"Who precisely?" casually, I ask.

"Black women preying on white men, that's who!"

"Where there's demand, there's supply." I return.

"That's just grand, isn't it?" slowing down her walking to tag her British to Irish.

"Most of who you see are married," she says like a tour guide. "And I mean both the hookers and their clients."

The Thames turns around with a disgusted face as she is quickly leading through the bar from one short end to the other, "It's interesting how much a man will pay to get into a woman's knickers, isn't it?"

I say nothing, especially to the white men wanting to pay to have black women. The black women paying with their bodies to house white man's money. Somebodies trying to be nobodies.

At the Irish pub, most of the patrons are bellied Brits, and of course Irish. Immediately, I hear rowdy laughter and broken glasses once the pub darkens. Many of the men at the tables have Filipinas and other Asian women with them. A group of women sitting in a quieter corner sips on glasses of wine torturously. So deliberately slowly. So many words come out instead, as if they are tipsier off of them than the wine they are gently drinking—than the wine they are womanhandling.

White uniforms slide in between customers, waiting on their patrons and shoving overpriced drinks to poison down their overworked souls.

Beer prices are heftier than many New York City prices. We order regular stouts at the bar. The bartenders are South Asians. They serve us both very large sizes. Thames goes on a back and forth civil argument about the dimensions, but mostly about the miscommunication.

I just watch in silence. Bartending is a tricky profession. A hustling vocation. The bartenders seem to be composed, too collected, too confident to make such an easy mistake. They are hustling Thames, and they are doing it in her residential backyard.

She gets perturbed and says, "Just bill it to my business account," flashing a plastic gold card. She does not look at the breakdown of prices, signing away monies and payments as if they were mere numbers.

Even the servers are South Asians or Filipinas. They float around invisibly, much like how manual laborers in the Gulf attend to menial work, but they are intentionally overlooked, because their presence may disturb the illusion that the hosts and professionals expect to work for and live in. In automaticity.

How is this place Irish?

River Thames is getting drunk. "You've got to hear this band play," she says in her robotic, mechanically tightened British voice as we sit down at the bar.

There is a table of Asians near us. They have four tables put together for their large group. The men are mostly thin with intensely bright, buttoned up polo shirts, hair sleeked and parted, and black-framed glasses tightly hanging on their faces. In the center of the table is a bucket of ice with nothing else in it. The group is boisterous, especially the men. The women are slouching off their seats.

"Those are tourists from China," Thames says. "Flocks of them visit Dubai."

"How do you know they are Chinese?"

"Manners," sipping on a new mixed drink, a gin and tonic. "That's how one knows."

Cheers come from near the stage area where the band is playing.

"They're excellent," in her slight drunken stupor. 70's rock and some 80's retro blast off, British style. The guitars are flaring away, the vocals barely audible. One of the guitarists pulls up his guitar to stress the strings, frenzying the people standing just below the stage waiting to make their dance moves.

Few older women dancing in the crowd go nuts, screaming broken words of alcoholic defeat toward the band. The guitarist gives them a boner, an extended guitar note as appreciation.

Not one man is dancing, though.

Most of them near the floor are hunting women, scouring the domain and waiting to attack their prey. Two large male bodyguards stand as pillars on each end of the stage, there to probably protect the women from such men, but more perhaps to protect them from their own sloppiness.

"Aren't they spectacular?" the River softly lays. Her gluey, dark brown, hybrid eyes smolder into me. Her drunkenness is heightening rapidly. I am casually sipping on my beer. Casually sipping what I see all around more than what I can barely hear coming out of her.

River Thames draws closer and brushes her palm on my thigh under the table. Then she tightens it enough to get my full attention. She breathes out a cocktail mist of hot alcohol into the side of my face to whisper, "You, suur," pausing slightly to look at the band before turning around, "r a FUCKAH!" she says with eyes rolling back into her head, in a slow, privately marketed way of seduction, wrapped in a half-numbed smile.

I take it as a compliment. "Fuckah" coming off this woman's lips is an invitation, a direct invitation into what makes her so dynamic, so difficult to pierce, when she is otherwise sober.

"FUCKAH, is whatch u r, isn'tit?" she tags her question with a statement first, as Brits so unnecessarily do.

I smile back into her words, smiling especially heavily back into her mouth. Dark hair, dark eyes, a dark and richly intelligent personality all beautify her. She is one gorgeous woman, certainly for her age. I invite her endearing term and say, "We'll soon find out what sort of FUCKAH I am," winking at her, "won't we?"

A "Pleeaase do!" slur barely comes out intelligibly.

The band is average, but in this part of the world, the types of bands may be seen as extraordinary. Dubai, like Kuwait, does not always get the best attractions, but they sure know how to hype up prices for second-rate entertainment.

The next day, we take a taxi ride downtown into the old areas of Dubai. The taxi driver is wearing his seatbelt and he is using signals to change lanes with a very stress-free nature, in a very stress-free environment. The ride is comfortable. Dubai is comfortable.

The streets seem quiet. Empty. Vacantly rich. It has to be because it is the weekend. The sizable force of manual laborers need to rest, too, yet quite a load of them are out chasing the chimera of money.

Money is the fool's gold that traps most people. The ones who create money believe they have enough power to enslave others into sub-social classes, but do they realize they are entrapped by their own creation? No master can exist without a slave. No slave can exist without a master. Each exploits the other. Both spend—waste—themselves trying to live up to, for, or without the other.

We drive past some of the old markets and Tims points to some blue-glassed buildings and explains how fantastic bargains can be found in the backrooms of such places. The salesclerks, supposedly, are eager to escort interested buyers to back doors and alleys to show them earthly paradise filled with the most material pleasures. Knockoff bags and accessories are what Thames usually rummages for. The Italian imitations are a fraction of the price of the originals, she tells me.

She would never live in this area, even though the apartments are much cheaper. I ask her why and she says that the standard does not suit her. So I ask her to explain what she means by standard, and she says she would rather be close to other Europeans. Down here, the buildings and markets have aged. They are situated in the city's pit, a place that many would rather stay away from if they could. People here can not afford the lavish lifestyles of Dubai Marina or Jumeirah Lake Towers, places built on excessive desire. The people in these areas have let go. Not necessarily given up on life. They have let go of the chase because it is out of their grasp. The ones who can migrate up the ladder probably face more personal sacrifice, more compromise of their identity than the ones who remain still in their content.

Most Dubaiins try to get into the newly developed areas because people who aspire for the things that are new and shiny are finally able to afford and waste more money on luxuries that counterfeit the soul.

"Give me the change and keep 10," she says to the taxi driver. Thames seems to always tip her taxi drivers extra dirhams. Always tipping everyone for services rendered, even though prices here are already idiosyncratic.

We are dropped off right next to Dubai Creek. Old mud and concrete alleyways have been turned into hip cafes and art galleries.

Tourist groups pass us.

Tourist traps are waiting for them.

Tourists are snapping away pictures at the architecture and ambience. Dried mud walls and simplistic living are seductive to the over-technologically strained societies of first world countries, the nations that proudly call themselves developed. Civil.

Some of the European ladies are speaking in Italian. The temperatures are pleasant, somewhere around 24 degrees Celsius, or 75 Fahrenheit.

Fahrenheit: Celsius. Celsius: Fahrenheit. Shit! I get mixed up the more I travel.

Few women are trying to ward off the sun by wearing wide hats and shawls. Many other tourists are plump and stop every few minutes, pulling up their faces to lay them barren to the sky. They sigh as if they just received closure to something. What they are really doing is letting the sun bask them, tan them to a shade that is not naturally their own.

How interesting to see Caucasians leave their cold and sunless winters for countries that are warmer so that they can turn into a color foreign to their own. The dark-skinned ones seek to be whiter, paler. The pale ones seek to be tanner, darker.

Both are enslaved to the other's natural skin.

It is Friday and almost noon. Most shops close early because it is a day of gathering, as the day of the week suggests in Arabic, and it is a day of prayers. Meaning, many true practicing Muslims will be flooding large symbolic mosques seeking guidance from imams, mostly seeking to wash their weekly sins. By true Muslims, I mean the poor and uneducated. Manual laborers. They are the foreigners from India, Bangladesh, Indonesia, and other overpopulated and impoverished nations who clean, cook, and cater to Arabs and other more privileged foreigners. To usually more privileged Muslims.

A small squadron of thin Pakistani men walks in packs towards a mosque. They are readying to submit to Islamic call of prayer. Most of them look at Thames' cleavage passing by. Few of them suddenly turn their heads toward the ground, trying not to soil their Islamic beliefs as they herd towards worship. That is how one knows they are heading to a mosque. Many stare at Thames' tattas and probably over-imagine what it would be like to touch such milky, silky skin. It has to be more pleasurable compared to the menial work they probably deal with for long hours without pleasure of the flesh.

"Cover the tattas, goddamn it!" I whisper to her in a stiff tone to what the French refer to as "tits." "These men are raping you with their eyes. Raping you with their imaginations." I shove my preaching into her.

What women may not understand is when men stare at women's sexual parts, they are not only objectifying them, but they are taking pieces of a woman for their private musing, taking chunks of a woman's core trait for a temporary and fleeting pleasure, stealing a vital essence to use for a passing thrill, like a postcard.

It has nothing to do with insecurities. It has very little to do with control. Nor does it have to do with power over another. Respect is the answer. If I have earned to be with a woman like Thames, if such a woman has invited me into her most inner fabric because of how I can make her feel, because of what I can allow her to become, then skin should not be shown so openly for others to steal away in a moment's passing.

It should be earned through suffering. Through dedication. It should be earned through enduring personal exposure, like I am going through with her.

We are animals at our core. No matter how civilized we like to believe we are, we are animalistic. Flesh turns on other instincts that we have to normally hide just to appear courteous. We have to deactivate our sexual impulses for a religion. We have circumcised our own pleasures by placing rules and regulations on them.

"You have no clue what goes through a man's mind," I flick at her.

She does not do anything.

"It's *your* body. Do as you like with it."

"You have no idea what goes through a woman's either," she protests. "You can't talk to me like that! I'm European. No one talks to a European woman that way."

"I just did. Cover them up."

I do not expect her to, but she out of the blue pulls out a shawl from her bag and covers her shoulder area, including the damn tempestuous cleavage. She seems to despise my supposed manly control, yet she seems to also respect it.

"You are too Arab for me." She pushes.

"I'm nobody."

"I knew it. You just can't let go of your Kuwaitiness, can you?"

"Yet yours wants to show itself," I flick back at her. "You could have ignored my request and done nothing, but you chose to cover. Explain that!" I try to look into her sunglasses. I try to look through her European and Arab senses, trying to get deep into her womanhood instead of just merely depending on nationality.

More streams of Pakistani men channel through the narrowed alleyways. I see her being overwhelmed by their manliness. Their testosterone. I take one of her hands and pull her hard into one of the European art galleries. Then letting go, I free her into her comfortable space. "It's for your own good." Freeing her into her supposed free European womanhood.

We go through a tight corridor which leads into an open café in the middle of the place. They have taken the central open courtyard and replaced it with a coffee shop. The main water fountain that used to be the focal point of the indoor Middle Eastern garden is tucked in one corner, making room for tables, coffees and their connoisseurs to sit and sip while gleaming over their mobile phones.

The place used to belong to a Persian Emirati fishing family according to one of the descriptions on the wall. Now, it is a Western art gallery slash café serviced by Filipino and other foreigners from the East. Foreign concepts serving foreigners by other foreigners, all inside what was once a local residence. This is a live art gallery in itself!

The traditional rooms now house paintings and other

forms of visual arts. Few of the paintings are about women's identities with Dubai's skyline in the backdrop, cosmopolitan women from first world countries who are seemingly trapped by an Arab city's modern desert. The paintings are of colors and senses snared by illusions and mirages.

A mixed media portrait in another room shows a young British couple dressed in suave clothing, with fit bodies, with glimmering white teeth and polished hair. They are nervously grinning at a child to their side. The child, who is being raised by an Indian nanny, is plump and too clean. Too perfectly clean. She is closely hugging the nanny while crying and screaming out of fright at her parents.

This is true Dubai.

Meandering slowly up the stairways, we end up on the rooftop. The same establishment has modernized it with comfortable ground cushions placed against the walls, lounge chairs, and vertical vegetation to oxygenate the area when Dubai gets sticky during many months of humidity. Few of the old rooms have been changed into event and office spaces. There is one room that is a library in the making. Most of the books are written by foreigners about how to escape to and understand living in Dubai and the region as a whole.

Books written by foreigners. For foreigners.

Where are the locals? Why would tourists want to buy books that other—resident—tourists have written? Their stories would not be the same as people who are actually from here, how they perceive their heritage and customs in relation to temporary residents. There should be citizens who write about how their city is being invaded by alien herds.

I guess that would not be a popular idea because it would probably not sell.

The art is in the pitch. Anything could be sold if it is pitched charmingly enough. Emiratis should write about how Dubai is slipping, losing its history as a fishing village to foreign acculturation, and they ought to write it in the language of the invaders: English. Would such words not sell then? Surely!

Thames and I tour another gallery. It is another old house caught by artistic modernity. Old Bedouin sadu cushions take up one's eyes. Abrupt paintings about selfhood echo off the walls. Vegetation rests in between. Reprocessed, wooden, and paneled window frames invite but square and close off rooms. No one else is here but us. No individualities are here in flesh and blood to peruse other souls caught up by multiple cultures, caught up by various personas.

The art seems to be staring at us, testing our understanding, testing our sense and limit to become the art by looking at ourselves through it as a mirror. "How much would you like to know? How much can you allow yourself to know?" is what it is saying.

So I stop. I pause my body movement. I throw out my headlights—eyes—to travel into one painting. The shape and meaning are abstracted by thick, jellied white and blue paint. The deeper I look, the further the shape appears to be a shadow of a being, silhouetted by a genderless body. It is sexless. There are not any male muscles. There are not any female curves. There are not any open seclusions pointing to a male or female.

Walking through more tapered streets, I force Thames to stop at a cut off alley. Nothing is at the dead end besides floating leaves and tiny pieces of paper. The light at the end is a shadow, throwing off most of the sunlight that breaches the other areas nearby. The walls on each side stand in great, whitewashed height. But, the end corner is breathless. No tourists try to go through it after seeing its end, its rubbish. Thames does not see what I see, and she tries to hurry me to move on to the next tourist stop.

The end corner is not an end. It is a beginning to an end. It is the only photograph I take downtown.

On the other side of the path is a modern poster encased in a bus-stop glass container. Nothing else is around it. It stands above asphalt and between concrete, held up by metal and glass. The sign is just words. It reads:

WHERE IS HOME?
I DON'T BELONG HERE OR THERE.

We finally end up behind the century-old Dubai Grand Mosque. It is located right on Dubai Creek. Most of the earlier Asian men we saw have congregated there, talking to each other before washing themselves to go into the mosque without their footwear.

On Dubai Creek, one water taxi is hurriedly moving passengers from one end to the other. Every single commuter on it, including the driver, is very dark-skinned. The large tourist boats waiting at the banks, however, are more littered with white skins.

The creek's currents look powerful, much more like a river's.

Since it is Friday, many of the dark-skinned are snapping pictures of themselves and their families, radiant white teeth shining through, for simple jubilance.

Thames and I reach an open area off the banks. She does not seem to know where we are exactly although she has lived in Dubai for many years. There is a squarish open area. It is just open pavement. I can finally breathe a little from the tight alleyways.

There are stretched out, horizontally white and red

railings containing many of the water-taxied darkies, who are prodding against each other to move along in a long twisting line. The railings end up at a tight doorway hurried in one of the old walled structures next to the Old Souk. In their finest clothing, routine worshippers are all heading into what a sign says is the Shiva Temple. All of them are about to submit their sins for quick absolution.

"I never knew!" River Thames exclaims, finally changing the tempo in her voice from a monotone commander to a more sympathetic little girl. "A Shiva Temple in Dubai?" like her heart just sank.

She seems to be lost in her own residence. Thames seems to be a resident tourist in her own home. A home that is not her own.

A residual tourist.

Who knew Hinduism would be allowed to prosper so openly and right next to a large Islamic mosque in a cosmopolitan city, in a region closely associated with Islamic practices? Shiva, known to be the creator and destroyer—the transformer—is right next to a vigorously flowing Arab creek, right next to an adamant religion that strongly goes against statues and multiple deities.

As she is looking over the worshippers lining up, hand gesturing, bending their bodies and bowing going into the temple, I pause to look at Thames instead. Who is this lady? The curves of her face reveal so much honesty, because there is no other makeup but eyeliner and her infamous lip gloss. She is not even wearing her concealer today, where she dabs a little to accentuate the darker parts underneath her eyes with the rest of her facial skin.

Who is this lady who wears her hair out, covering so much? Bangs and highlights veil grey hair, veil grey matter underneath all the external hair and skin. Is she a woman hiding a little yet revealing so much at the same time?

On the outside, she appears collected. In control. But, I catch her at moments when her truer self comes out in weakness, unmasking and inviting to validate her not simply as a multicultural entity, nor simply as a woman, but much more as a living organism defending herself and celebrating what she perceives as a truer form of life.

She is aging the best way she can in the midst of other aging figures. A human humanizing herself the best way she can according to truths that befit her the most, that befit her the best. Thames is like Dubai Creek behind us, flowing and sustaining others for its strength and beauty, yet rarely are the uglinesses underneath seen and appreciated.

This woman is hosting me in a city she has recently called home but is just another temporary destination to her. She is hosting me with so much energy, with so much selflessness that one must take a protracted closer look to better understand the dynamics of why such a woman—being—gives and shows herself in such ways.

Past the temple is where the Old Souk starts. Old wooden door shops with frankincense and other aromas linger against bright fabrics and sugary Arabic pastries. Smells and colors that intoxicate and hallucinate. Wooden designs arch against mud-concrete walls. Arabesque lamps hang off shaded ceilings while saris, pistachios and turmeric glitter momentary walkways, where souls come to pass their breath, where souls come to trade themselves for other transitory pleasures. With other transient consciences.

Again, tourists are bombarding the place. Most of them according to Thames are fresh off the cruise ships that dock nearby. They intermix with many of the South Asians who live in the city. It is odd. It is like how the adjacent Dubai Creek's currents meet each other at the Arabian

Gulf's outlet (or inlet) with varying temperatures and strengths that crash at each other. Crashing for one another. Crashing because of the other.

The souk is supposed to symbolize Arab and Iranian traders who bring their goods to sell and barter. I could not spot one.

Not one!

Most are Pakistanis and Afghanis speaking to fair-skinned tourists in broken English. The darker locals—South Asians—rush around the lighter tourists. Everyone rushing through everything and everyone else. It is an organized mess.

It is like River Thames.

Like me.

It is getting too hectic. Thames begins to breathe heavily, fidget her head. She sees me doing something similar. It is as if all the tourists, all the people who are moving through one person's arteries, are depleting their purpose of sustaining their host. These cells are swimming through, adopting their own selfish faith while occasionally paying homage to their supplier when they seek redemption. A transient redemption to their benefactor. A residual redemption to their simultaneous taker.

I ask Thames to go somewhere else to have lunch. We hop in another expensive taxi and go to Burj Khalifa and the Dubai Mall. Along the way, I glance out to the ships coming in and going out, to all the people and products being imported and exported. Landscaped trees and flowers groom many of the main roads. Perfectly marked road lanes keep people uniformed.

"Give me the change and keep 10," she says again to the taxi driver. We are dropped off in a car park in one of the less frequented buildings adjoining the mall and heightened structure. A mother in an abaya and her son are anxiously waiting to take our taxi right from us, to perhaps hurriedly go to another borrowed destination. Locals like Thames use these back channels to stave off the influx of tourists treading locals' sanity.

Before getting to the Dubai Mall, we meander through smaller malls. The stores promise endless happiness. The shiny stores are hospitals for addicts, the very same junkies they help to create.

Shit! The Dubai Mall is beyond huge. It is spectacular. There are so many shops, so many choices, so many consumers. Franchises from the UK and US dominate and have come into another developing country to culturally colonize and Westernize it to death. They are here to warp people's perception of individual culture and nationalism.

In conglomerates we trust!

There are too many people. There is just too much buying. Everyone is in a rush to go up escalators to try clothes that do not suit them, to accessorize their bodies with false impressions, to order fast food that hurts more than nourishes the body. To get a temporary happiness built on illusion.

Everyone is in a rush to buy things that are unnecessarily expensive, unnecessarily replaceable. It is a craze. People look deranged and hypnotized. Their souls have been pulled out of them. They are zombies moving around aimlessly, purchasing and snacking on temporal pleasures, chasing the delusions of love and happiness more than ever attaining and holding on to them.

All I can see on salesclerk and consumers' faces is buy. Buy. Buy!

Please, DO-BUY!

This is DU-BAI for you.

Here, it is not so much one's skin color which shows

distinction. Here, one's paper color reveals division. This place is a museum of the obsessed. A mausoleum of the possessed.

A fish restaurant that sits right in front of the dancing water fountains is where we decide to lunch. My entire body, but specifically my mind, is exhausted from the endless images of purchasers gathering things they barely need. Products built to amuse a person into temporary bliss is not happiness. It is an illusion. A fake rush. A ploy to hypnotize the masses into thinking they are productive workers who deserve salaries to buy shit that is quickly replaceable. Replaceable products are always upgradeable, like humans who upgrade their partners to reach a temporary bliss called love.

I let River Thames go and select fresh catch of fish from inside the restaurant to have fried and grilled. She is a very devoted and hospitable host. She is also a very devoted but selfish, domineering woman.

The water fountains are about to start. The railings along the walkway swell with people suddenly. Local Emirati music begins. It is the only local song I have heard since arriving. Many men in the song are singing proudly together in a traditionally Bedouin, low tone of voice, showing uniformity—showing much less individual ego. I can visualize it. The men are squeezing tightly together, like many Levant dabka dances, with arms down unless one is lifting a sword or twirling some type of significant knife. White smiles mesh with glossy eyes to sing a very tribal, a very patriarchal song into tradition. Definitely, into history.

Not one voice is a woman's.

A photograph of an Australian holding up a large fish on a private boat is on the front menu. The caption reads he was also responsible for having enough passion to open a varied fish restaurant. I look around to see what is taking Thames so long. I only see Arabs and Filipinos running the place. Running the other joining restaurants, too.

A few young women are snapping selfies in front of the fountains. One is a blonde. Another is head veiled. While one more is dark-skinned. Heads pointing up in the air or tilting to the sides, asses bumping out into passersby, and lips pouting into their phone's cameras. This is the new trend. Advertise who you wish to be but are not in reality. The women are tapping on their screens, probably filtering themselves so the rest of the world will know who their alter egos are once they post.

Where do chunks of one's identity go once photos are taken? Do they reside in infinite space, robbed of the person in the photo, or do they collect in parallel universes? I have always wondered where parcels of people's collected self go once they are adopted by digital photographs that are sent into the cyber world. Into a cyber cloud of a collectivism.

In democracy we trust!

Is this why ordinary individuals would rather live online than in reality, because it casts a variant self, a different version of themselves than what biology and environment have presented as reality? Online women and men are goddesses and gods boosting their worth otherwise bland in real life. Mascara, lip gloss, foundation, treated hair, and muscled smiles are filtered into superheroes, into alter egos that seem to seek more recognition than simple living, than uneventful, menial truth.

That must mean I am a Menial. But, I am definitely not a Millennial.

In lies lay many truths!

The River comes back, but the orders take too long.

This is a five star restaurant. Why would it take too long? The place is not crowded. Who exactly rated it? It will be going down a notch if we have our say.

The mezza comes way too late. Hummus and other smaller dishes suddenly flood the table. Pickled cauliflower and olives spice up the half dishes, the Arabic appetizers, the mezza. When the fish comes out, it is presented much better than it tastes. Plates holding up other white plates. Shiny cutlery wrapped abundantly in insulated napkins. Sets of over-cleaned glasses positioned behind one another. It is too organized. It is too refined. Too much of an illusion. Too Dubai.

Presentation hides so much.

Truth is in the substance.

Both of us pinch away at the mezza with Arabic bread. Then we utensilize the fish, chewing each bite steadily, making sure we head tilt while taking in the food, making sure we are as presentable as the cutlery to enjoy our momentary diversion for the sizable price that will be paid. Less guilt will be felt as a result.

Two Emirati men in their upper 30's or 40's with young warped-faced women in their mid 20's sit at the table behind Thames. One of the men is very good looking. Sleek grey hair, sharp cheekbones, semi-pointy nose, a fit body, and a quiet but confident voice make him stand out. The other man is not as attractive. He smiles too much into the good-looking man. Kissing ass does not bode well normally. Not an attractive quality.

Both women look average. Cosmetic surgery can only beautify so much.

I do not get it.

Why would an attractive man need to be with average women? Sex! Why would a successful-looking man want to be with fake faces?

Money buys as much of an illusory fetish as it begets it!

The two go hand in hand like water and food. What you earn and spend is the quality you make and exhaust.

But then I do get it. Personality is always changing. The two women with pointy noses, puffed lips, colored eyes are avatars, are the new facially veiled niqabs because truth is not enough. Truth is not appealing enough. Not beautiful enough to cater to a growing sense of shiftiness, to a growing sense of multiple difference.

Personas are always updated. Always upgraded. Touring.

"What are you thinking about?" she asks. "You seem preoccupied."

I do not answer her with words. Instead, I lurk into her eyes, searching for an explanation to why she would ask that. She does not flinch. Calm and inviting, the River allows me to flow in.

"Why divorce?" She quizzically asks. "Why now?"

I have to remain silent for a minute to grasp her words. To grasp her eyes diving into and throughout me. I have to ask myself the same question to know why any man would want to pull away from a union that he got himself into, that he chose to create. And why would any man want to depart his own flesh and blood, little children who ask the same sorts of questions when they want a pure truth, especially from the father who seeded them?

I can not help but allow myself to crash in front of her. Tears start wetting my eyes. My cheek muscles start to break. I can not easily stare back into this woman. A woman who I dated as a teen. A woman who I took the virginity from. A woman from my far past asking about another close woman from my recent past.

I feel stripped. I am caught between women. I am caught because of my pasts. I am caught because of my chosen options.

I feel residual.

A real nobody.

You're trouble!" She smokes out, while her eyes sizzle at me every now and then, as we are holding hands walking ever so slowly through an insulated monorail bridge, holding hands through a trance. Our fingers are walking, feeling, exploring each other's skin texture, one another's fleetingness. We are exploring each other's flightiness. We are exploring gripless permanence.

People are flooding to Burj Khalifa, heading hurriedly toward gluttony. People are passing like phantoms, sliding through us because of fixated agendas in alternating dimensions, and taking glimpses of us without asking. They are taking glimpses without caring. They are definitely doing so without knowing.

"Trouble!" Again, she breathes out, torching herself, assembling a world into one word. Assembling one description that would eventually bespeak both of us.

We take another taxi and wiz it to an art complex. "Give me the change and keep 10," she says to the driver.

Alserkal Avenue is in a rusty industrial area of Dubai. Where art space meets art food, the enclave houses contemporary artwork that takes on musical ensembles and creative play at food design and dining. We wander from one gallery to another, visually tasting each place's sense of artistry and architecture, nipping at plant-based foods and drinks—drowning in all the creativity of the area.

Dubai is opening up, artistically. It should. Instead of depending so much on material gain, it has redirected itself into the art world to harness consumerism.

This is how I view it anyhow.

Even though art tends to bring out individual thought

through creation, the result is to sell the craft at ludicrous prices, much like other products in spouting markets throughout the city.

But, none of it compares to the artistry of Thames. A simple T-shirt, curve-hugging jeans, basic flat shoes, almost no makeup, and a quiet body—with the occasional smile—bring out a mobile artistry, a mobile and live perception that none of the business-oriented places can offer.

She is a gallery of galleries.

Through her eyes, a bible of energy that words can barely pay justice to comes out. Textures of emotion, fabrics of devotion, waves of humanization come out. I see her as the teenager. I see all that she has made the woman she is.

Our steps are courteously slow, weaving in and out of the different exhibits, paying more attention to how our hands caress, smiling into one another because of a strolling injection of lust wrapped in ecstasy. We are both high. We are high off one another. All the art around us only elevates it higher.

The outcome is abstract.

This is my final day with her in Dubai. I have to go back to Kuwait before flying over to the US. She is grabbing as much of my emotion as she can. She is taking as much of my character as she possibly can. Leaving a footprint is vital to a potential monogamous relationship, even if we live in two different cities, countries, and slightly different cultures.

I sense Thames wants to harness what never had a chance of continuing when we were teens. I sense the River wants to stream all the energy she has collected through experiences of making other men succumb to her to finally succumb to where and with whom it all started.

At one of the eateries, amongst replastered and redesigned décor, I leap into her abyss. Her eyes are dilated. Awake. Yearning, like a little girl's. I start talking to her eyes without speaking. The plant food is presented so aesthetically, but the portions are controlled.

The prices are another story.

I continue softly lunging into her collected being. I move into her mixed and cultured personality, her personality of mixed nationalities, rebellious gender, shifty cultural identities, and I spew love.

Love. Love in the moment. Love for the moment.

I choose words cautiously but do not overthink them. They come out because they are made for her. They are made right here and right now. Thames deserves them.

My ego is not in the picture. It has been let go who knows how far back since coming in contact with her again. I throw her words of artistic emotions, words that help to define the vitality of the art all around us, words that artify her in the midst of them all. It all heightens her into a new potential identity that should have been done ages ago. Heightening her into a woman she should have lived out when I first met her.

Her silence is wordy. I can sense so much in her quiet eyes. They are pleading to be taken and sustained, like I would a daughter. Like I would a mother. Much like I would myself.

The only emotions that seem to want to come through her eyes are tears. They are tears of accrued salt that have waited to be proudly recognized, and freed. In them, I do not see what I have had problems with, which is monogamy. In them, there is not any classification or categorization that I have to worry about being trapped in. In them, I sense a full and deliberate surrender. No monitoring. No control of one another.

I sense I want to give her myself.

"Am not interested in getting involved with anyone," Thames says with a painful voice. "I need to free myself from the hell I have been in and start my new life."

I do not flinch. I just take in her real words that are coming out through her eyes, instead.

"Don't worry, I am not pinning my hopes and dreams on any man and you are quite safe from my clutches," she throws out to test my reactions, like women often do by using reverse psychology, regardless of which culture, country and city they may dwell in.

I am still silent.

"Ok, just don't go falling in love with me cause it will be my turn to break *your* heart." Her stiff London accent is defensive. She is scared. I do not think she has ever truly fell in love and stayed in what she fell for. She is finger rolling her paper napkins, leaving a scrappy mess. The rest of her body is poised though.

In control.

Yet, without it.

I finally break my silence to exclaim, "There must be a reason why you are letting me in like this!"

"When you figure it out, let me know, because I don't." Her head moves up into the vertical plants hanging from the ceiling. The café is one of many trying to teach, and sell, sustainability. Green vegetation comes down from the ceilings, comes down from Dubai's skies, coming down to kiss a dehydrated desert floor. The artistic youth are introducing sustainability to the old, most of it is in deeply insulated, air-conditioned bubbles.

"If you don't like it, we can stop," she says, breaking my shifty thinking, "but I enjoy hearing your voice."

Again, I am silent. This woman has not earned her position as a chief executive officer among men at a large logistics company for being gullible or naïve. I am silent because she is cunning. Masterful. Conniving, using her soft, physical attraction as bait when delivering her mechanical and monotone British accent. She is constantly clever. She is constantly sustainable.

"Don't you have flings? Not even ones you meet on the Internet or sext with?" she throws to tempt me into revealing more about myself, but it is an attempt to cover one of her residual insecurities.

So I cave in to see how she responds to my contaminated honesty, instead.

"I just got divorced," telling her but telling myself more. I look at her pupils, throwing what remnants of honesty I have. "I'm just trying to take care of myself," confessing more to see how I respond to my own pity, which is consistently in turmoil.

Thames waits for more. She is not satisfied.

"I want quality," I lay out candidly.

Being alone is wonderful but difficult at this age, yet I seem to need someone of worth to validate my existence when no one else could do it with the aptitude that I desire.

I continue and say to her, "I want a companion. Yet I don't want traditional monogamy. I like my mobility and space. But, intelligence and elegance matter. There are women I've met, but I don't have the inclination to invest in them. They are not worth the time."

"I am sure you will find the right companion who shares your values, eventually," her eyes diving into the table, losing hope.

She pulls her face half way up and says, "It takes some of us longer than others."

"Doubtful. Almost every single woman I've ever met has gained more from me than vice versa. For a woman to upkeep me will be incredibly difficult. Plus, women, like most prospects, are fleeting pleasures."

"I like it when you are honest. You want a companion but don't believe you will find what you need."

"There are good women that I've met, but they fall short of knowing how to mentally, spiritually, and emotionally sustain the relationship they mutually want to manifest. According to them, I'm just too complicated. They are just too plain."

I may be too complicated for myself! Is this why I am on the constant move? Is this why I tour cultures, sightsee places, vacation in others?

"Oh dear," she whispers out like a mother.

"I don't fit conventional molds."

"I can see that."

"I am a free spirit living for the moment," I send into her, "because that's all there truly is."

Thames looks distracted. But her eyes are gluey. Adamant with desire, her soul just stares, just eats into my craziness. This woman does not take anything too lightheartedly. When another can possess her, how ever short, she is religiously engaged. Those eyes are the proof.

I tell her, "For this reason, I'm alone most of my life."

"Better alone than with the wrong person," volleying back. "I do not seem to be able to commit to anyone anyway, so I am not hoping for a relationship," her voice changing intonation, into a little girl's plea for help. Then River Thames switches gears and stiffens up, "My attention span has been very short in the past."

"Being alone will tear you initially as you let go of spatially close comforts," I attempt to reassure her soon after her divorce, soon after displacing herself once again after touring one man to another. "It will numb you, but your weakness will be your strength."

"I am ready for it."

"There was so much lust before between us. Two wild forces intertwining to unknowingly create a greater hurricane," I throw at her.

The food is finished. Much talk—much honesty—has been revealed during one meal. Heading out and into other galleries and event spaces, we relinquish our egos and allow other people's renditions of truth through art to shape us for a while.

Few of the artists expose pain caught up by surrealism. Of the pieces, few have large elephants photographed under road bridges in destitute African countries.

In black and white.

Many of the black Africans in the photograph are not even impressed. Their hunger and exhausted souls look like they are the animals domesticated by a wild elephant, as if they are animals in a zoo.

As we are about to leave the area, I spot a huge sign above the entire district reading:

WHEN WILL YOU RETURN

Jumping into a taxi to head back to her place, River Thames holds hands but will not look at me. Her calm conduct looks out the window towards Dubai's very organized and clean streets.

"I want you to heal me," saying while staring out into the maze of roads. "I want you to feel what you missed," moving her head even farther away and into the flushed, luminescent skyline, "so that I don't feel worthless. So I stop repeating the same patterns."

She finally turns and says, "Maybe you were my first and you will be my last, before I give up on men and sex."

"Why are you sending all these?" I ask about her messages, not sure why she is bombing me with a British band called Keane who sings and lyricizes with meticulous agony.

"To explain how I feel. I am in self-destruct mode."

"Enjoy it, alone," trying to stall her charade of self-implosion.

"Ok. Two can play your game."

"Enjoy it."

Posts about my books that she has reposted suddenly disappear on Instagram, shutting me quietly out of her short-lived, alter-egotistical life online.

"That was infantile," I reply. "I just don't like to follow anyone!" I explain but testing more her latest mental and emotional chess move to see how much I would budge without needing her; without caving in my caveman sense of emotional, devout connection to her.

"Why don't you block me as well?" I tempt her urge for deconstruction. Detachment. Destruction. "Do it! I triple dare you!"

"I'm sorry. I can not be who you want me to be," referring to how I have lately asked—pushed her caressingly—to hide her deep V-necked T-shirts, which flaunted her cleavage for prying, horny male eyes, especially East Asians laborers.

"You want me to cover myself, not show myself and be loyal to you, while you do the opposite. Is that why your ex doesn't have a profile picture? You told her not to?"

Accusatory sewage spews out whenever fear takes her over.

"Nobody tells me what to do. NOBODY!"

She is on a roll. I can not halt her progression to askew me. Askew us. Abort us so immediately. I do not want to stop her from killing herself in the process.

"Nice fucking earrings you gave her by the way. Fuck this. It is warped. Forget me," marching her commands of weaponized kill.

I send her an emoji of two hands peacefully coming together to what may appear as respect, but also prayer. I submit so she can continue her self-sabotage that compels to break and sustain herself. It is the same sabotage that has sustained and broken us.

"No. You don't have a clue. I see that now. I love you. But I should have never contacted you. And opened this Pandora's box. I can not cope."

"Fuck you!" I lay out in an infantile show of hurt.

All she responds with is: "Good luck - fuckah!" A term of endearment that we have used to define our recent behavior for one another, a compassion and growing passion to uphold each other with respect. Honor. Divine submission. "Was fun while it lasted . . ."

"You are a mess. You go from accusatory to apologetic in minutes. You make endless empty threats to leave, to only reel back like a lost puppy. Mess!"

"Forget me then. Go to one of your easy, tidy American pieces of ass. I am a mess by nature - Palestinian Austrian Kuwaiti British."

The taxi driver looks and acts like he is going through meth. Missing teeth, wearing a black beanie over his eyebrows, and laughing boisterously, I have to help direct him when his driving is sporadic. Acceleration and deceleration come and go like a song's verses.

Fuck, no one is on the streets. It is 2:30 in the morning. Just let me catch my Lufthansa flight safely.

He stops at a gas station, leaves the meter running, goes out of the car to pump his own gas, starts arguing with the attendant whose sole job is to pump, making me pay for his indiscretions.

After the expensive gas stop, he starts turning up Egyptian music. Satire is part of everyday storytelling in Egypt. Definitely in songs.

The song describes the hardships of living in slums, notably Cairo's main cemetery called the City of the Dead. The place is four miles in size, and people who are alive actually live amongst the dead there. Many choose to live closely amongst their departed.

The song hilariously mocks how the same government representatives who help to remove the slummed out Cairenes—Cairo residents—from developing areas also live amongst evacuees, all of them living side by side and on top of each other amongst the dead because of bureaucracy and corruption.

Manshiyat Naser, meaning Garbage City, is the most impoverished slum in the city. A lot of Cairo's trash ends up in that parcel of overcrowding. At the same time, much of the same trash is collected and reused.

The singer jabs at how so much wealth is found in the waste by garbage people called Zabbaleen, who are mostly teenage and adult Coptic Christian men numbering in the tens of thousands. He sings in a heavy melodramatic tone of voice. He picks at the government, provoking the powers that be with the use and lost art of retaliation. It is hilarious. Ingenious. Honest.

Living in, and as, so much trash saves people from unnecessary spiritual corruption when they are otherwise consumers being consumed by their own lifestyle.

The taxi driver rolls down my window in the back without asking, increasing the song's volume. His cigarette hangs off the side of his face while his torso is tilted forward close to the steering wheel, checking through the rearview mirror and chanting the song's lyrics.

It is as if he is the singer in the song.

Zigzagging smoothly in and out of cars, he asks where I am going.

I tell him Germany. Actually, Frankfurt is just the transit point to the United States.

"When you come back, call me. Inshallah, I'll pick you up. You'll get a good price, inshallah. You're family," he says because we are residents of the same building. He laughs and then rambles about German soccer teams and players. Then he starts talking about individual goals and trade payments clubs make to acquire and release players.

He is shouting all this as his right hand keeps increasing and decreasing the cemetery song. And, as he sings along, he is dancing his shoulders and smiling his eyes through the rearview mirror.

Now, the other window in the back is rolled down. Cold air storms through around the back of my neck. I do not want to catch a cold, specifically before a long flight. It would not be a good sign. I ask him to shut the window since he has both in the back child locked.

He closes it, but soon he opens the front passenger window.

"Guten Morgen," he says in German, saying good morning, as he peers back with his nose and eyes through the rearview mirror.

He pulls back and talks to himself, testing out words and phrases. "Guten hilwa" he morphs German and the Arabic "hilwa" to mean in total "good beautiful." A few laughs steadily jog out of him, amusing himself mostly.

There is some residual logic to his hybrid "Guten hilwa."

I turn away and look out into the streets' darkness. Street and car lights radiate specific areas, giving supposed life to individual pockets of darkness. But, all lights lead to darkness. Without blackness, light would not exist.

Up and down, the windows and music and storytelling suddenly make me burst out a laugh with him.

I give in.

I surrender and decide to let go of myself.

I just do not care anymore about self-composure. Kuwait has messed me up. So have women.

After hearing me laugh, after seeing that he has a receivable audience, the taxi driver goes nuts and accelerates the car, accelerates the music's volume, and accelerates his stories. Windows still gyrate throughout the cab. More whispers of half phrases and embellished songs of agonized humor roll out of him.

I finally begin to understand.

I finally begin to see him. He is not a machine for hire. He is a human man who needs to cleanse himself in the craziness that his job, that this world may inflict upon us. Through his taxiing, through his spiritual taxiing, I have come to realize that we are all insane because we try so hard to compose ourselves not only for a world impressed into us, but for a world within that we have helped to ruin us. All because we want to think we are sane.

We are all garbage men, recycling.

I tip him well.

———

At a business airport lounge in Frankfurt, there is snow gently gliding down on to dark tarmac outside, finally finding destiny after falling for so long from touchless clouds. An espresso glances, allowing its steam to belly dance the beginning of my jetlag farther. Deeper. Much more earnestly.

Outside the front doors of the lounge, I see aluminum walls with shadows streaming in a hurry, coming out of a gate and heading to another point of assembly.

Inside the lounge, people are snapping pictures of objects, of themselves amongst Christmas trees, carefully positioned foods, and dexterously placed smiles. This is the new generation of photos doing the talking. Sentences, paragraphs and books are not as necessary anymore. Post photos and let the viewer personally interpret them into phrases, clauses, and if lucky, a few sentences. Attention span is shorter now. Who wants to read a few hundred pages of well-crafted paragraphs? So much is on the go. Take things as they come. And take them as they go.

Residual tourist.

River Thames' latest message screams. It is assembled in a jumbled knot of emotion, in exquisite senselessness.

"I didn't go to work today cause I'm a mess. I need to talk to you. Can we speak while you are in the lounge? I don't want to lose you, but I don't know how to cope with you. With my feelings. I keep trying and failing and making us both miserable in the process. I want to resolve this before you get on the next plane."

I just observe the screen and decide to call her. I want to hug her spirit back, back into this fiery but embracing wired mess we have caused by coming back together after nearly three decades of decadence and bodily and mind intoxication that dealt with self-sabotaging our unique energies, which has only required mutual acquiescence.

Understanding. Validation. Deliverance.

She calls the meeting fire igniting air. Air oxygenizing fire.

Again, there is no solution. Just more mess. I hang up.

The last message I get is: "You're the unhealthiest relationship I've ever had."

————

I am seated in the back of the plane. Sleeping is a challenge. On and off dozing. On and off waking. I do not know where I am anymore. I do not know who I am.

I am renting a seat for hours, enclosed by two armrests and temporarily hibernating souls; it is a small compartment of space that must be endured for a limited time, much like a persona. Trying to escape would exasperate it. Yielding will gradually transform it into another persona.

Two American women are standing a few feet behind yapping away. Is the stereotype true? Are Americans boisterous when they travel to other countries? Their topics are matterless.

I detect loneliness.

I get up to stretch and to get some water, drawing near and talking to them about crap. They just left a tour of Morocco and are going back to Denver and some tiny Rocky Mountain city. The large woman is overfriendly, on a plane loaded with Germans and Arabs and few German-Americans who choose to be in-betweeners. There is talk of the solitude-inspiring Saharan Desert, old markets loaded with spices, antiques and their pickpockets, endless dark red teas drenched in saffron, and tall handsome Moroccan men in the mountains with their jealous village wives. Other talk is about a young Afghani-Brit male who loved to take off his shirt, clearly making these older women nostalgic.

They are exchanging the Rockies for desert. I am

exchanging the desert for the Rockies.

I tell them I come from Kuwait. I give them the pros like an overpaid prudent ambassador would. They are both in their early 40's. Not sure why people in America normally look older. It is partly their over-hormonal, processed fast food. I tell them I am older than them, but they think I am lying.

Why would anyone want to age himself?

When they both ask what my star sign is, I tell them I do not get into Western star signs as much as blood types. The robust woman says her blood type is AB-, the rarest.

It is never a coincidence when negatives meet.

The shorter, snowboarding woman in yoga pants says she does not know hers. Most people in the US do not seem to know. It is hidden from them. In Kuwait, it is written on the back of the civil identification card. I get into the facts that have recently come to me about negative bloods. How they are a minority in this world yet rule it. How this world is not what it seems.

"Want a calf massage?" Snowboarder asks. The woman has an ass on her. Her face and hair need attention. What I mean by "ass" is not too male looking. This one has curves that I grew up with. Something to latch on to during turbulence. Something to pray to during self-doubt.

"Yes, please!" to the massage.

She starts twisting and turning at my calf. It feels confessional, like I want to submit something. Maybe a hidden half-truth. After she finishes, I give her one without asking. Her eyes role.

Heaven just struck.

She says she has never married or had kids. She is not interested in lies. My type of woman.

"What's missing?" staring into her to see how much she can gush out.

"A partner."

"Companion?"

"That's a better term for it. Yeah, companion. What's missing with you?"

"Companion." I tell her. "But a woman can be a mess."

She laughs. "We're all a mess."

A flight attendant comes and whispers that we can not congregate in threes or more on a plane heading to the US. "American regulations," she says facetiously.

That fucking harassing Haras.

We exchange numbers. I want to unravel this woman, the boarder out of the snow.

Or is it I who wants to be unraveled and leave behind pieces without ever wanting them back?

COLORADO

L anding at Denver International Airport, I wait in a long swirling line of internationals. I wait in a long line of screening. In a long line of vetting.

The line is moving much more slowly compared to the other line for US citizens and residents. Over there, some are speaking English. Others are talking in Spanish. Few in Arabic. They are all seeping through America again, after their international travels, to dilute the US into a growing nation of obscurity.

The United States does not have any official language. That is right! None. Most Americans do not even know it.

Some in line are young adults wearing sweatpants and hugging teddy bears. Baseball caps worn ghetto style, tilted and purposefully messy to seem street. They hold on to bulging and sleepy, warped eyes due to jet lag.

Most of the other transients are glued to their phone screens, tapping and adjusting letters, tapping and adjusting words, tapping and adjusting identities.

Partitions and ropes are opened and detoured by TSA representatives. People are divided and led through them like vehicles in traffic. Individuals go through printing parts of their spirits in a momentary line of movement.

Impermanent but touristy.

One of the TSA personnel ushering arrivals in dark trousers and a blue shirt is standing still, having her legs in an A formation. She is positioned. Grounded. Her voice is authoritative, directing and dictating to the internationals who have come from various countries in Europe and the Middle East. Directing and dictating to the internationals that they have landed as new personas in a new land, on a different continent. They are welcomed to a varied reality.

Under different sets of perceptive laws and regulations.

My turn comes up. The customs agent motions to move forward with two of his fingers. He asks routine questions about why I am here. His voice is mechanical. His training has been effective.

"What is your purpose in the US?" he commands.

"Leisure." I pitch back with a dead face, pronouncing the "ei" in the word as an "e" while the "r" is negated. It comes out more like how the Brits would pronounce it. "Leja."

"Place the fingers of your right hand on the pad in front of you," he points to the device on the counter while he types letters, numbers and identity classifications to see what sort of persona he can electronically find.

"Place the fingers of your other hand." His fingers tap and push across his keyboard, searching and assessing a selfhood of me according to probably political and economic affiliation.

"Look into the camera straight in front of you," he says next.

I look into it, smiling my soul away.

"How much money are you bringing in?"

"9999 dollars," I tell him. "I'm here to spend money. To help out your economy."

$10,000 is the declared limit.

"Whose address is the one listed on your entry form?"

"Mine."

I see him losing a little of his mechanical, facial composure, so I say, "It's my holiday home."

Suddenly, he looks back into the computer and types faster. Clicks, spacing, and returns later, he looks back at my face. This time it is human, personal.

"It says here you were a US citizen."

I say nothing.

"Have you forfeited your citizenship?"

I say nothing.

I know he is not allowed to ask about such things. It is none of his business, not part of his fixed, job description.

"As you can see," I tell him, "I am a Kuwaiti national."

He just dives into my eyes, erasing everything and everyone else around, as if his eyes are the only things I see, as if his training is the only thing I am allowed to sense—compute, waiting perhaps for me to slip.

He gets none.

Tightening his jaws, he punches down to stamp my passport and hands it back like an android.

I respond with a soft and humane, "Thank you."

I am back in the US after a few months of absence. I was in Kuwait after a few months of the same. Back and forth between Kuwait and here, and other parts of this divided but fast, integrated world, I am moving while collecting. I am collecting while dispensing parts of self.

We are all cars crashing into each other to create various matter after we are partly destroyed. When we smash, we create. That creation then diverges. That result leaves a footprint behind, but it continues touring. It continues evolving. It seems to want to always continue adapting.

In versatility lies stability.

The baggage terminal is organized. People are waiting to pick up their luggage, waiting to pick up parts of themselves to readapt back into a familiar environment.

Here, space counts.

Each person gives and allows an arms length distance or more. Individual worth matters. Individual integrity is crucial to an overall sense of freedom. My TSA approved luggage, which permits them to use a master key to open it, awaits.

No one is that free.

In the Middle East, closeness is part of the norm. Being nosy pressures individual behavior to be subservient to a collective good. To be subservient to uniformed traditions.

Loose jeans, breathable shirts, and droopy facial cheeks speak to personal comfort here. Cars and large portions of food also speak to proximity. Even though many may not see themselves as dressing in a uniformed manner, like dishdashas in Kuwait, it is fairly easy to spot which generations of clothing fashions come from; thus, making it easier to see uniformity according to generational distinction.

I finally see Irish honking at the arrivals just outside of the sliding doors. Her face is so fresh looking. Little makeup. Rouged cheeks. Blue eyes piercing through. Perfect teeth on top of a mountain-fit body, and intensely healthy tattas conservatively hidden under a turtleneck.

Those tattas can feed a whole impoverished clan of kids.

"Trouble's just landed," she yells out the passenger window. "Hi habibi. Hop in." She is wearing kohl eyeliner all around her light eyes with dashes of mascara. "I've missed you so much. Got so much ghee waiting to be churned," means Irish is horny and needs to be serviced. Properly! And tonight, no matter how jetlagged I may be.

I taught this woman too much about the orient.

"Miss Colorado?" turning her head completely for an answer.

"Why else would I be here?"

"Ghee?"

"So I flew 10 thousand miles *just* for ghee?"

"Special, all natural Irish ghee. Nothing like it in the East."

"True. That's worth thousands of miles."

Along I-25, there is so much space. Cars respect proximity. European-apartment-sized pickup trucks are everywhere. They love their trucks huge here even if the prices of gas are higher than Kuwait. Still, gas is cheaper than in Europe; hence, the popular compact cars over there.

The air is bone chilling, crispy cold. The Rocky Mountains in the distance appear majestic, magical; they are calling me back home. They are calling me back to a home away from another home. A home away from several homes. A home away from a part of myself.

She says my place is stocked with food, bed sheets washed, rugs vacuumed, floors polished, and the heater is on to make any jetlagged man comfortable. Once I get settled in, she wants me to go to church with her. Church has been her go-to refuge.

"Inshallah," I tell her.

"I hope that's not the third inshallah," states Her Irishness.

"I taught you WAY too much!" I throw at her. "Please focus on the road."

Colorado is always calming. The Front Range's mile high elevation clears my mind and soul to understand myself the best.

Personal space is respected although it can create loneliness for many. People want to be touched and validated for their special self-made worth, but loneliness often kills them. The middle of the two is residue, a space that can trap many souls if they allow their own desires to overtake them.

"Still got women at every port?" she shifts.

"I don't know what you're talking about. Words are my women!"

She always—yes always—interrogates my fidelity when I come back stateside, or when I come to be with her at the end of the night after going through other souls who seem to also search for the same thing. I have always made it clear to her that I ultimately belong to myself, not to another person. Never to the same eternal yearnings but more for the hunger of living in and for the moment.

"Oh, I'm definitely taking you to church this Sunday. We'll see what happens to your word mistresses. I'll have pancakes, Italian coffee, orange juice, butter and jam toast, and lots, and I means lots, of ghee ready for you, too," she teases knowing food always emotionalizes a man's stomach, "unless you prefer kayaking?"

"I surrender," cutting off what will be paragraphs of expected duties she thinks I will fulfill if I protest at all. "Anything but kayaking. We'll go first thing to church Sunday morning."

"Inshallah, habibi," Irish giggles and throws a small plastic bag of dried fruit into my lap. "Chew on the dried ginger. It'll help your jetlag."

"Oh, great! I just got inshallahed by an Irish woman. I taught you too much. WAY too much. You're a mishkilla, Irish."

"La, habibi. Ana hal." Irish says in a twisted American-Arabic accent to indicate "No, darling. I'm solution."

That I did not teach. Damn Google!

She is becoming a problem (mishkilla) who is going to outsmart me soon. Irish is going to herniate me. That is what happens when an older man dates a younger woman in her thirties. They do not put up much of a fight at the beginning until later. Much later. Most of them are single mothers and hornier than jalapenos. After they saturate you with tons of ghee, they then learn and consume parts of your personality so much that they can turn it all around on you when you least expect it.

In the American vernacular, it is called pussy whipped.

They can become you and throw love and other shenanigans right at your face, tiring you out gradually. What man wants to fight himself at this age when butter-cream comes from a beautiful younger woman? With matronly Irish tattas at that?

Not me!

Where am I? I wake up and realize I am on a roomy king-sized bed. How long have I slept? It is Colorado. Just like that and I am in another country. Another time zone. Some other reality. Just like that I am in someone else, touring through another personality. Just like that I am another borrowed person who will embrace others, as they do the same to me.

I pull up the window blinds and see pure white. It is snowing. A few trees are lit up. A snowman stands with a carrot-stick nose and red gloves. Sidewalks shoveled in a well-mannered way. The whole neighborhood is happy white.

Happy sappy happy.

Every house has a garage. There are no wires dangling from any window, no cracks on my walls, no shitloads of honks 5 in the morning for no apparent reason, no sounds of heavy furniture movement coming from the family living under me, and I definitely do not anticipate any wallahis coming out of runny mouths.

Alhamdulillah.

I go downstairs and see Irish preparing something.

"Here comes double trouble. Good morning, Mr. Snores."

"How long was I out?"

"15 hours straight. You snored like a bear. It was cute."

"What's that smell? It's damn good."

"Mosey down next to me. Here are the ingredients to homemade apple pie. Mmm," she whiffs out. "You'll love it. Everything is fresh. Fresh fresh fresh. The eggs are from a woman I work with. She raises her own chickens without any pesky chemicals. Her daughter brings them round every week. A woman I camp with makes this wheat flour right outa her little cabin up in the mountains. Isn't that nifty? I hand-pick the berries," pointing to the bowl with a large wooden spoon. "Everything is nice and fresh. Mmm."

Where am I? Did I wake up on Little House on the Prairie?

I try to sneak some berries and she slaps my hands. "You're trouble, mister."

"Why am I trouble? Because of a few berries?"

"No. You're always trouble. You always approach a situation or enter a room with your feet first, not your head like most men do. They safeguard themselves. It's very difficult to reach them. But you, you come with slight vulnerability, which women adore. Women like men who are a little vulnerable."

"Me, vulnerable? Never!"

"You are, habibi. You use intelligence. It has very little to do with your looks. Intelligence and vulnerability are important."

"That makes you want to change us?"

"No, it makes us trust you easier. Trust you with our complex emotions."

I have nothing to say.

"I'll massage your head, back and calves with essential oils when I finish with the baking, ok? I'm going to be taking good care of you while you're here. You were a very frustrated, knotty mess in Kuwait," she says frowning like a mother to a child into the flour bowl.

"Naughty? What did I do this time?"

"No, silly. K-N-O-T-T-Y knotty. The other naughty will be going to church tomorrow to wash him of his Kuwaiti sins."

I see her sipping from a tiny shot glass. "What are ya drinking?"

Mild eggnog she tells me. "Tis the season to be jolly, la la la la, la la la la."

Is it Christmas already?

I must be in la-la land.

Writing can sometimes be dreadful because it is constant homework. There is so much editing, adjusting and overlaying of technique. Most of the time, however, it is thrilling when the material I use to write is about experiences I undergo personally.

Research!

The experiences help to transcend them into a play of words and sentences, genuine play at punctuation and capitalization, flirting with the actual memories and transferring them into a collection of chapters in a hopefully colorful story. The idea is to conclusively create a unique consciousness. The purpose is to manifest stories worth reading and remembering, giving rise to a life worth living.

———

Ace Gillettes is an underground jazz bar in the pit of Armstrong Hotel. Fort Collins' older and established personalities frequent the joint. Jet lag and a tequila high allow my Buddha to smile, to steep out of my face, out of my soul.

A young female bartender shows off her skills by neatly pouring stiff alcoholic drinks, with fruits and syrups, to civilize the poison to her older clientele. Tips are the goal. Greater confidence, the greater treasure.

Behind her, chaperoning her moves, is an older bartender. Preachy words come out of him to mostly the females, who are trying to act classy; meanwhile, he preaches colored potions of alcohol, keeping the dames illustrious. Settled. Yet hypnotized.

The sax player pulls in, up and out various chords. The cello player massages a tamer melody in sync. The pianist straddles them both, knocking and mocking their chords by infrastructuring them to keep mesmerizing the women and men into nodding, into following their every chord. Into following their every orchestration, like devout followers of faith who seek communion. Affirmation. Resurrection.

I purvey the dark room with my quiet presence. I survey the different entities that have come out to be entertained. I study the souls who come out to be heightened.

Research!

Most are couples. They are chained to marriage, to a contract they had no inkling of comprehending, when they probably used to be carefree, when they used to be careless, when they most likely cared less.

While I sit at the bar, I peruse the different women. Most of them are parrots talking to each other, casually flirting with their drinks, throwing eyes in corners, nodding at most things they listen to from their partners yet they can barely hear because of the loud jazz pulling at and pushing into their egos.

Behind, I see this dark-headed woman with strong facial features. Mediterranean. She definitely looks Mediterranean.

I see her energy flipping and flopping with a woman next to her who has reddish-blonde streaks. I give her a light look, a look of raw desire. Raw earnestness. She gives back a look, but I break away, scrutinizing the other people. I stare at the other souls of the night, out and about to release themselves from their routines, who are about to release themselves from their habitual hold.

Tattoos drench a plump redhead next to me. The tattoos are typical designs and colors of fantastical creatures and lost loves. They are cries to be acknowledged and validated; however, they appear to be shallow advertising done through supposed art so the inner soul, the inner being can be decoded by one, just one special entity who can appreciate such a woman—human being—for living through this earthly realm looking for light, hope, and love.

Vanity.

Her face is instantly familiar. She is a barista at one of the local coffee joints in Old Town. There is not any makeup on her face. Just freckles. Colorado women can be plain. Earthy. Organic. They can also be eternally abundant, internally.

I look back at the dark-haired Mediterranean, smoking into her eyes, not getting webbed by her flashy, trophied teeth.

She waves.

I look at her for a few seconds, turn and look away, thinking she is flirting with her aura probably, and she probably intends it that way, to twist and torment men into lusting after her. I glance back again at her dark complected aura. It is powerful. Inviting. Too perfect.

She finally calls me to come over to her table. I do not budge. I only sit here. Something makes me not want to move. Have I had it with women and their antics of allure? All for what? Sex? Just so that I penetrate their vaginas when I would most likely provide the most tantric sex that they have ever had? It is just too much work for little reward. Or, the reward does not compare to the headaches I would receive by dealing with their fluctuating mess.

All women I have met have been a mess.

Mess!

All of them.

I am no picnic, either. I am perhaps a bigger mess. Divorced. Constantly streaming through countries and cultures. I am constantly surging through women, constantly streaming through their complications yet rarely settling to appreciate what an art form of a mess they can be. Rarely do I sink into their hormonal imbalances that most men barely comprehend.

My own mess would not help a constant mess. Two continuous messes do not equal a positive, stationary mess.

She comes up to the bar and starts talking. The usual introductions begin. Names, bits of smiles and laughter, and the eventual head tilts come out of both of us. But mostly her.

I skip everything and ask where her name comes from. She classifies Mediterranean and Middle Eastern countries according to how I facially respond. In respective order.

Italian, a touch of Greek, Palestinian, and Egyptian flow out.

She is not Egyptian.

Her eyes are Greek to Palestinian. The woman is an array of cultures, drowning and becoming what she sees fit for a particular moment.

She smiles and flashes in maneuvers, eventually pulling me back to her table. I sit next to her friend who is very pale in comparison. Her face is composed of very green eyes, hair in red overdrive, and skin masked in ivory.

I start talking to her. I do not ask for her name. Ginger, as I would like to call her, just looks at me. She is staring deep into my eyes. I feel a tingling sensation. Her eyes do not blink; they just persist. I gradually soak into her. She smiles, but they are smiles of nervousness.

Grand trust flows out. Grand trust is absorbed the more I talk.

The Mediterranean woman eventually slides next to us. I order a Fat Tire beer.

Strong local beers usually allow me to diversify senses of myself, alcohol fermented in a localized piss-colored drink and chilled to a perfect degree usher a more fun-loving persona.

The Med starts brushing one of her polished, fingernailed hands through her silky hair. The other hand is playing with her crystal necklace, aiming it at me to have it test my energy—my sincerity. Back and forth, flipping and flapping hair, she starts revealing she is Palestinian. From Ramallah.

The place is a tiny Christian, agricultural sea village in the West Bank just outside of Quds, or what the Israelis and the West prefer to call, Jerusalem. It is known for its olive trees and mountainous height overseeing valleys towards the Mediterranean. Muslims now outnumber Christians there.

"Ram" is height, while "Allah" is God in Arabic.

The Ancient Egyptians and Crusaders conquered and religiously used the area, while the Ottomans made it part of their empire centuries ago. Christians succumbed to Muslims. Muslims succumbed to Christians.

Brits governed over both during World War I. The Pals rose against them during World War II. Jordan then annexed the Pals' land in turn. After that, the Israelis took it over without granting citizenship to Ramallah residents. More rebellions ensued in way of Intifadas. Israeli walls then divided similar cultures.

Religion and politics divided peoples. Their identities have been caught, exchanged and buried so many times in between and far along.

Here she is. Palestinian-American, following many like her family who fled to the US to escape a constant flux of identity and dogmatic confusion. Here she is, a melting pot of history. A blend of East and West. An America.

The lounge is ebbing and flowing. A group of elderly couples dressed in suits and flowing dresses starts to leave. Young hipster men in skinny jeans topped by over-bearded faces slink off the edge of the bar. The beard trend resembles Middle Eastern men who have long worn it. Now, it is facial couture in the West, when many here have been brainwashed into thinking Muslims are enemies. Yet, they wear beards like them, eat their hummus and smoke their shisha in popularity.

Hilarious.

Finally, I start talking about negative blood types. Ginger says she is AB negative. Palestine confesses she is O negative; both of them negatives without knowing about each other's special blood type. They examine one another, baffled at their unique blood. Baffled to what it all means.

I take smaller chugs of the Fat Tire even though I constantly see the waitress smile some pressure into finishing it. Back and forth, she streams through, not waiting like a good waitress should.

The two negs start talking to each other in whispers. Then O- moves in closer and starts flirting with gentle words.

"I have your book. I saw your pic on the back cover."

"Which book?"

"You're a writer, right?"

"Sometimes."

"Is that your pen name?"

"One of them."

"What's your real name by the way?"

"Nobody. With a capital N."

"Anyways, I held your book in my right hand. Something about it made me want to hold it. I didn't read any words. I borrowed it from that local Arabic restaurant near campus and took it home for a day or two. I just held it. There was something saying to me to want to hold it."

"Ever return it?"

She avoids the question.

The second beer is taken away prematurely, but I realize it minutes later. The waitress is probably conditioned to do it by the same lead bartender who has taught the junior ones to always keep the drinks flowing. Even if the drinks have not been finished yet.

We head out. The temperature is chilly. Med begins talking in a Palestinian accent. Then Egyptian a little. Then

American English, belly dancing abstract descriptions of the cold. Her faces pouts and she rubs ever so gently her stomach, her curved gorgeous figure against my manhood as she describes her stars.

The first tree the two see, they hug. They pour their energies into another spirit. They energize their own in turn.

A pipe comes out of Ginger. She lights it and tokes in with an earthy smile. She holds in her breath, exhaling her calm being out to me. Pal snags it from her and swallows her own version to give herself a high, detached from the jazz atmosphere we all just left behind.

The smoke high is a new chapter of the night.

We stroll down College Avenue. We finally arrive at one of the squares. Red and Ramallah are dancing and twirling, rejoicing at their own energies that seem to have just recently elevated—liberated—them from much sorrow. They start screaming into the star-filled sky, the moon.

A homeless man packed in unmatching attire yells back.

Red goes and hugs him. Together they come back and join us. West Bank tells him he is a beautiful soul. She pulls out a large yellow crystal, puts it in one of his hands, and wraps it with her energy. Love.

Then Occupied Palestine and Gingerly both ask the homeless man what his blood type is. He shuts down. His energy breaks, away. Silence. He is eerily silent. Not one word comes out of him, and he takes a few slow steps back, glaring at us with fear, "Are you witches?"

Both blood negatives say yes.

He dodges away into a corner and vanishes.

West Bank asks for my address. I give it to her. The night is young, and the moon glancing down tells me to take this woman further. Deeper.

The Arabic kohl eyeliner, which is where the word coal comes from, is dangerous. Delicious. Scanty. The way it hangs all over her top eye hauls me into her inner world. It wants to pull in and probably sink me within so she could chew my energy and spit out what is trash.

I know. I know because I do the same thing to women. But, without wearing the eyeliner. I just wear and flaunt myself. Unmade up. Pure. Devastatingly honest.

Eyeliner is worn around the eyes so richly. Deeply. Handsomely hypnotic. It is hard to look away from her captivating almond-shaped eyes, her soulful trap made up with dark-snaring eyeliner. I am sure she knows the power the eyeliner emits. The power her Arab booty nets. She is seduction.

Yes, the noun "seduction" and not the adjective "seductive." I only go against grammatical protocol when I am blown away, when I am "seduced," or when I want to contest something. Or someone. It is an amusing form of self-intoxication.

We drown a few shots of tequila at my place. The sensation of feeling half numb and half awake is delicious. I pull out some raw Palestinian zaatar that I brought back from Kuwait. I even bring out dirty Palestinian extra virgin olive oil. When she sees the zaatar, she loses it. The thyme, sesame seeds and sometimes sumac mixture that makeup zaatar produce a light and flavorful spice. Arabic bread, or pita as locals call it, helps the taste bring back pleasant memories of the Middle East. Taste of strong herbs on brick-oven baked bread unleash Arabism in her.

"This is the earth I miss," saying while eating lipfuls, olive oil moisturizing her soul, herbs pilgrimaging her back to her Palestine, roots that not one Palestinian I have ever met would not go back to if they could. If they were allowed to without being criminalized.

"Deliciousness," she says while going to the fireplace and doing yoga stretches, pointing her gorgeous bulging ass toward the triangular vaulted ceiling. "Life is deliciousness." Perfectly thrusting her ass—curves—at my face. Deliberately making me salivate at her goddess of a form.

She is wearing a pendant with the all-seeing eye, the eye of Iris. This woman looks reptilian. A reptoid. A shapeshifter. She looks like a lizard in human form. Her cheekbones are sharp, pointy. Her eyes are almond-shaped, snaky with a venomous look to them, as if they are out to charm their way into everyone—everything—they encounter on their path with irresistible love that would take much more to get out of.

An Om tattoo on her right wrist sticks out. Half of it looks almost like the capital letter "E" in reverse. Much like the Arabic number four: ٤. Actually, numbers used in the West *are* Arabic numerals.

The Solarium is a hostel located in Old Town next to the university campus. The temperatures are moist and the whole place feels tropical inside, with lush trees and other rich vegetation coming out from corners. Hence, solarium. Zaatar has invited me to have dinner with her and some other people she would like me to meet.

She is not around when I get here. Instead, Gingerly is waiting with her usual bent smile, not sure if it indicates happiness or nervousness. Both.

She leads to the kitchen and introduces a middle-aged man who is cooking some shish kebab, heavy-duty chicken, and concocting some frozen salmon over biscuits and pickles. He has a very pleasant face, a very welcoming baby face, with a cap over black-framed glasses and a red flannel shirt. The skin on this man looks very soft, like he has eaten organic fresh food for long periods of time. His smile is very hospitable. I shake his hand and he tells me to go ahead and indulge in whatever I want. I wait for others to show up, though.

Ginger Ale leads to a map on the wall of northern Fort Collins with the Solarium as the focal point. I recall reading how many people have disappeared around parts of northern Colorado without a trace. Could they have been rhesus negatives who were sucked through portals or taken by government agencies for hybrid experimentations? Rhesus negatives are half alien and the new version of humanoids. Most of the individuals I meet in Colorado are from these minority bloods. It should not happen because they are so scarce, but they often know their negative type of blood. Positives do not seem to.

Ginger Ale also points to an adjacent map of the world where travelers have come. Some come from faraway countries like Kazakhstan. Others are from the very eastern regions of Russia just above Japan. Most of the travelers come from the United States, however. She finger points, "This is where she has been."

"Who?"

"Ramallah."

"Really?"

"But this is where she wants to go," sticking her finger to Palestine. "This is where she *must* go."

Soon, other people start coming into the kitchen, to different food that is cooked. Ramallah is part of them. A man looking in his 40's quietly leads in with a tight baseball cap. Ramallah asks him how his day has been. He has a bent American accent, bordering on Northeastern to Midwestern. She asks where he is from, and he says

Chicago. He then talks about Turkey, how he has lived there for 8 to 9 years.

His accent points to Israeli. It is hard and harsh. Ramallah gives me back a look when I think that, as if she telepathically knows he is Israeli. We sense he works for the Mossad.

Negatives are high empaths. They are also incredible telepaths.

Another man—40's's or so—is an electrician down from Denver. "Denver is terrible compared to here," he says casually, his face faded—weathered-looking like his clothes. "I've been to numerous hostels around the world, but this place has got to be one of the best."

The cook nods in affirmation.

The cook was in the army for many years. He had enough and left to travel and explore the world. "I've gotta pick up this '78 Saab from Colorado Springs in a few days from an elderly gentleman who has the thing parked untouched. Just left in the garage covered for years.

"I want to bike with a friend across northern Spain, along the Camino de Santiago Trail. Walking and hiking that would kill us. We want to take our time. Feel the place." He moves around the large wooden, cedar-looking table to one of four fridges and pulls out a Corona. Snaps open the bottle, leans back on the main counter and says, "I've been to Thailand recently. It was a trip."

"In what way?" I ask.

"The place broods with soft contempt. Cheap women everywhere. Abundant booze. So much broken English. All of the white man's indiscretions came to that country to pillage it. Their beautiful women used our weakness for self-annihilation to their advantage. The sex trade is one of their biggest resources."

I tell him I am from Kuwait.

"KU-wait?"

"Know it?"

"Of course," he lays out, "I got shot there," he lifts the ankle area of his jeans, "in my left leg in '92," and jabs at a bruised area.

"After liberation?"

"Yeah. By friendly fire. That's what I remember about Kuwait," rolling back down his jeans. "You're from KU-wait, huh? Wow!"

"I'm actually half from there and here, but I've lost and found myself so many times over that I sense I'm from everywhere. More likely from nowhere."

"What is your name? I never got your name."

"Nobody. That's my name."

He laughs. "Most of us in this hostel want to be nobody. Were you there during the war, brother?" he continues.

"I was there during the seven-month occupation and liberation. I saw more than I probably should have. It was the best educational experience I've ever gotten. Mind-opening. It was definitely mind-blowing."

"War often is."

"Trauma often is," I reply. "The experience woke me to see this realm we call a world, to see this world we call reality in a different light. My perceptions are very sharp now."

We take our dishes to a lounge area in the actual solarium. The food is not that tasty. It is missing strong spices. Kicks that would open senses, unleash spirits. A young man joins us. He is one of Ramallah's kids. Her adopted kids. Her loved kids. His eyes do not fixate on anyone. A few murmurs come out of him to keep himself company.

Back in the kitchen, the Denver man tells Ramallah, "Remember that bright light in the sky? The one we saw a while back?"

"What about it?"

"It's gone. It vanished. It must've been a satellite. It must've."

That light is not a satellite. It is Nibiru. It has been coming back, and it is wreaking climactic havoc. From torrential floods and snow in deserts, frequent earthquakes in zones that should not see them, massive dust storms where there is no sand, and hurricanes and tornadoes in the oddest areas, Earth is going through change. This realm is altering. Not simply awakening. Altering. Many of the world's governments know of it, but they will not tell us. Instead, they choose to be accomplices in geoengineering weather to cover Nibiru's arrival. If one is aware of its existence, one should live life abundantly in the moment, for that is all that remains.

Life resides in touring the now. Now!

The tepee fire outside is lit. Different individuals are drinking. But they are smoking more. Plastic pipes come of Gingersnaps and this other man who has brought a jug of microbrewery beer. I take a hit first off of the man's tiny horizontal bong. He shows me how to block the small grooves on the left to get a stronger toke. Gingersnaps then unearths a ziplock bag of her own weed. She claims it is stronger. Purer. She finger massages a little into her bong and softly instructs me to take just one hit. Just one. It is that strong.

And, let me tell you, it damn sure is.

Alhamdulillah.

She just laughs into my face as marijuana smoke and the smoky fire from the pit begin to haze our senses. Giggles start pouring into laugher, defying everything a grown adult worries about. She soon joins in, and we both volley back laughs at each other, each one louder than the other.

Back in the kitchen, Ramallah is dancing and looking at every person, not only energizing their souls, their spirits, she dances around the kitchen through different inner beings, different consciousness. All the while, parts of her adopt the people she immerses herself in. I see her energize them, see her as the chameleon, a jester who fools and entertains nobility and arouses the commoners. She in essence mystifies the court, but privately she is someone who watches wisely instead of the foolish person a jester is often seen as.

———

The Alleycat is a mix of coffee shop, bar, and restaurant. It is situated in an alley just off Colorado State University's campus. Drifters and homeless from young to old go through this area. It is open 24 hours a day.

The two negs are sitting at the nearest table to the door. Books are all over the table with a laptop. The books are spiritually based. Other books are about tarot reading. There are different stacks of tarot cards, too. Ginger wants to give a free reading, inviting different cards to analyze me. She places certain ones out in the open. She says to pick one up. Then she looks deeply at me with her changing green to blue eyes, zero makeup on very pale skin.

I do not choose any. She is not going to trap me with cards. She should know better as a negative blooded woman. She starts reading some of the cards she put down. She is trying to cross-reference a unicorn one with a strong man writing over a stone fence. There is a fairy with a bow, too. None of these cards have any effect on me. They are just empty.

"Can I just stop you because they don't have any effect," I reverse it on her, and then she starts describing her situation involving her husband when she left Washington and went down through Utah to almost finish her tarot card license before arriving in Fort Collins.

How women can beautifully and abruptly shift.

She apparently was physically and psychologically abused. Many negs are. We may be feared for our power.

"Your presence is strong," she states. "Your confidence in others is as strong as it was at the jazz bar."

I glaze into her and reaffirm her confidence. She says I scared her when we first met because my energy was analogous to her spousal abuse.

"We are both negatives. I will never hurt you. I don't need to. We are family."

Later the same night, Med comes over to pick me up before we go back to the Alleycat. She rolls down the window on my side completely and locks it so that I can not roll it back up.

Is it déjà vu with that taxi driver?

Gusts of Nordic ice swamp my face, my Arab desert. She swings the car in the thick snow laughing her soul out. Then she takes a detour and goes to get tequila from a liquor store where she says she knows the owner.

When we walk in, I see pictures of him as a translator with American forces all over the walls. One in particular of a Hummer is spread next to the front door. The man's name is Haqi, and he starts talking about Iraqi proverbs much like a lot of Arabs when they talk to each other, using humor to relax and open their subject matters.

"I want something not too expensive, not over a $50 tequila bottle," Ramallah says.

She seeks some advice, but again with her, she can not decide. Smiling seems to be her only consistency, as it is a gift that emanates love, a powerful emotion she thinks has freed her of the physical abuse by the hands of her Palestine-American husband. Eventually, Haqi advises on a silver tequila for about $22 after tax. She hands him about $30 and then he gives her back the change. She says to keep it for someone who may need it.

"For whom, the homeless people?"

"Yes, give it to the homeless."

"Have you seen a lot of them?" he asks. "Most are overweight, they are not homeless. They're druggies." Haqi turns to adjust something behind him and then turns around, "Want to see homeless? Go to Iraq and see homeless."

She tells him there is no need to talk about anyone in a negative way.

He says, "But it's okay if they do when they come in here and start calling me a sandnigger? When I have 2 medical doctor degrees, pay taxes, served with the American Military, and got shot in the leg. That's okay?"

What is it with the leg shots?

Ramallah says, "Habibi, okay give me a hug." They both hug, but he can not seem to look at her for a long time, from one Arab to another. Instead, he makes another crack. She gives him heavier hugs and some sweet date clayja pastry she baked for him.

We leave and we fight off more road snow to the Alleycat. Going up the stairs, three different aged men are trying to bum cigarettes. Ramallah hands them out freely to each one. Barely anyone is in besides students tutoring each other and a couple of mothers, looking at their computers and cell phones. She talks to a good-looking guy with soft but sharp cheekbones who looks like a rocker from the 80's. He has a red bandana tied around his head. A Bon Jovi look-alike. I pull up to a table near the entrance. Bon Jovi tells us he belonged to a biker gang in West Texas. He keeps nudging at his red bandana, pulling it down to his eyebrows. Ramallah disappears into the lost souls, trying to bring them back to what she terms as "the light."

Jovi says America kills us all. "We pay taxes for working. We pay taxes for spending. Taxes for breathing."

"Those soldiers moved outta our way when they knew we came through," a young man says talking to another man behind us, who has his two feet on a chair, one arm lazying around it. "I was part of the special forces." A shumack resides around his neck, with his sandy military fatigues still wrapping his body like he has not left the Afghan and Iraqi deserts yet. A drained, indifferent face speaks otherwise. He is part of the other band of homeless apparitions that do not seek to be part of a normal functional society because he has lost hope after seeing—experiencing—disillusionment. After experiencing truth.

"I was born in Israel," he tells Ramallah coming up behind. "I've seen a lot. I've erased a lot."

His left hand looks tense. It is holstered next to his hip as if he is about pull out a large knife and slit something. Perhaps someone.

————

Ramallah rings the door, has a tall young man with her, pushes against the door and welcomes herself in, saying, "Get dressed, we're going down to Denver."

I can rarely pass up any adventure. It is in my spirit.

The young man looks 25. He is an AB negative. Half white half black. He lightly grabs her hand every so often while driving. Ramallah looks back once in a while and whispers, "We're just friends."

I did not ask and I do not mind. Everyone is a soul of their own making. Do what you please because everyone and everything is in the moment. Everyone is for the moment.

In downtown Denver's industrial gut, artisans and creative entrepreneurs have resurrected the area. Red brick factories, warehouses, and rusting train cars have been given light, hope to reawaken and persist again. Communal harmony is flowering the once graveyard of worked and sweated out souls for an industrial evolution. The energy is electric.

The youth are saving the aged.

Walking into an eatery joint that has been refurbished, reapplied, recommunitized, the establishment does not try to present the typical glitz associated with capitalist decor trappings of pristine moldings, unfaded walled colors, of mannequinned clientele and personnel usually presented like window displays. Of lies that many can never live by. Instead, reassembled wood, plastic sheathing, unprocessed metal, and raw employees have enlivened this junkyard—this cornucopia—this rebirth into inviting artistry. It has resulted in indulgent creativity.

A guitarist sits with one leg relaxedly crossed, playing something resembling Spanish Flamenco, teased with northern African—Arabic—strings. An orange wintery Broncos hat holds his head, elongating it and starkly contrasting the other parts of his clothes, which are typically black squared prescription glasses and a stylishly fit black coat with leg-hugging espresso jeans that are normally worn in Europe, normally seen in short-lived wintery Spain. His facial features are poignant, sharpened to approach this America with old country confidence. With old cultivated class. With century-old warred civility.

His fingers butter the strings. Each one caresses and teases the guitar in a suspended euphoria. His smile glazing along. Notes are brushed and held. Strings are loved and released. Painful and blissful emotions are captured in as much as they are emitted. I am hypnotized, embraced by his melodies, his ensemble of heart-warming and internationally diverse acoustics, in an area that was recently diseased by decease but brought back by temporal ease.

There is a paper-printed squared sign high above him in the shape and colors of the American flag reading:

IN OUR AMERICA ALL PEOPLE ARE EQUAL. LOVE WINS. BLACK LIVES MATTER. IMMIGRANTS & REFUGEES ARE WELCOME. DISABILITIES ARE RESPECTED. WOMEN ARE IN CHARGE OF THEIR BODIES. PEOPLE AND PLANET ARE VALUED OVER PROFIT. DIVERSITY IS CELEBRATED.

He stops for a break. I approach and talk to him, asking his nationality,

"Moroccan. You?"

"Kuwaiti."

"Ahlan," which translates into, "Welcome."

After telling me how he came to this land years ago as a student and married a local Hispanic woman, he talks about the corruption of Morocco. He talks about the close-minded justification of fundamentalist Islam, how a friend, for example, beats up his sister for wearing tight jeans and decadent tops in public. For Westernizing her traditional, patriarchally-made Islam because of the human yearning to be humanized in a constrained and fearful ideology.

He goes farther and reminisces about the bright blue stone homes, like the white Greek island houses that sit on sharp ridges with humble souls who knowingly live in poverty but triumph over it by living happily with their means. He also discusses how people back home are unlike Denverites who pay exuberant amounts just to barely be pleased, if at all. $3 is enough to party lavishly on a Moroccan beach, honeyed by free music from passing revelers, and deliciously accessible food by similarly impoverished yet impassioned spirits.

I join Ramallah at a gemstone store off of South College, a store filled with esoteric goodies. When I get there, I meet Yesadus, a blue-eyed Eastern healer. He is a self-named and self-labeled high empath. He hates most people, but he likes to channel people's energies from one plain to another. Channeling ghosts. Sifting and releasing pain.

Yesadus feels Ramallah's pain instantly because of her brother's death, who passed when he was four. Yesadus takes earthly, trapped pain, and his own existence, and sends it into the heavenly realm.

His eyes light up, his smile opening widely. "The two of you! There is something about both of you. Your energies are doing this to me. I haven't talked to people like this in a very long time. You two bring it out. Unlike my friends, they are closed even if they practice yoga and meditate."

I am quiet absorbing his jubilance. He glares at me with his happiness and says, "Your energy is something else. I see it around you. It's magnificent. Your energy is incredible. I use a scale to determine human energies and I'd say yours," pointing to Ramallah, "is around 400. His is above 500. Once an energy reaches 601, it becomes spirit form. It leaves the physical form. It leaves Earth."

He is so energetic. He is glowing. Flowing.

"I push dark entities away. Sometimes, I push them into the light. I believe in the goodness of light. They won't dare to come near me anymore. Light is too powerful."

"They are Jinn." I explain the Islamic belief of these intelligent beings of lower rank. They are spirits that exist in the same realm as we do, but only a few are able to see them. Not all of them want to harm. Most do, though. "In the Arab and Muslim world, they are a normal expectation. They live amongst us and we know of their evil intentions. They are normally understood as just superstition."

"What are they called again?"

"Jinn. J-I-N-N. The Western world translates the word as genie. As far I know, Islam is the only one to acknowledge them out of the three Abrahamic religions. It even acknowledges other forms of life. That can mean extraterrestrials. Aliens."

"Where are you from?" he asks.

"I'm from Kuwait."

He looks a little confused.

I continue, "I'm not an immigrant. Nor am I a refugee. I don't want to be American. I'm here as a foreign investor. Sometimes I jot a few words on paper."

Something made me just respond razor sharply. Why am I aging like this? Do I not care anymore for my own well-being? Or, I react like this because I do care?

He asks, "Have our American troops messed up Kuwait in the first Persian Gulf War?" He stares hard, trying to expel truth.

"Yes!" I say flatly, looking harder into his. "American lingo, your franchises and democracy have messed things as an effect. It's not really the troops, but who backs them high above that is misleading your troops into battle. Maiming. Death."

I reveal how many American veterans are neglected when they come back here. Lied to by the same people in power. Promising lower class Americans of free education, housing and other illusions. Killing them slowly is what realistically happens, instead. There are more suicides after soldiers come back then there are them being killed in battle.

Ramallah breathes a little harder. A little closer.

"I saw a man when I was in India appear after going through walls," he changes the topic, "change a glass of water like this one," pointing to his huge American glass of water, "and change it to something else like gold."

He shows an old picture of a guru. The photo is black and white, usually taken by lower castes in India, because they are poor. He looks like most Indians in Kuwait. Thick hair, oiled and parted from one side, with equally oiled facial skin, is an indication of sparse bathing.

"This man and that place changed my life. It showed me love. It showed the truest part of myself."

He leaves and comes back with a crystal. "This is for you," handing me a necklace with a beautifully laid dark green stone. "Put it on."

Once I do, a tingly feeling sprouts throughout my body. What is this energy? I feel at home. I sense this is my calling. I ask him for literature about the stone and he brings back a large intricate book.

The book writes that moldavite is an intense, dark green tektite stone ("molten" in Greek) of strong vibrational frequency that heals and protects emotionally and spiritually against negative energies. It is connected to interstellar travel and higher universal purpose, especially amongst star children.

Ah, star children. I am home.

It is a 14.8 million year old glass rock found near the Moldua River in the Czech Republic's Bohemia region.

"Is this where many Ashkenazi Jews derive from?" I ask myself.

It is made of a meteorite crashing into Earth's atmosphere, which is also associated with Lucifer's crown or third eye, or fallen angels who helped bring it down from the sky during the war between God and Satan.

It is also connected to Shiva's pearl brow, or third eye.

Is this why I stumbled on the Shiva Temple in Dubai?

Moldavite is mostly associated with the Holy Grail's nourishing spiritual and unearthly powers. Royalty have worn and exchanged it for its powers.

Wait a minute! From what I know, Jesus was rhesus AB- blood type. The upper rank of Ashkenazi Jews are mostly rhesus negative. Fallen angels, or the Nephalim are rhesus negs. Most European royalty are negs.

How many rhesus negative bloods wear moldavite?

———

Nibbler.

Spanish words come out of the two women. The second round of flat beer is dropped off by the young waitress. Boobs jacked up, ass thrown out, tats screaming in green and blue all over her plump body.

That is tats, not tits. The abbreviation and spelling are correct.

Alhamdulillah.

"Don't speak Spanish," telling them.

"He's a writer," Nibbler tells her two friends who are trying to deconstruct my intentions for their little Nibbles. "Watch what you say to him. You might be in one of his books." Her hair is so long, stretching all the way down to her rump.

Ball Buster says I look very Mexican. She is the hefty bulldyke Latina of the bunch. In Kuwait, they are called Boya, as in a boy-looking female. The blue-eyed Blondie next to her just laughs, speaking in Spanish until Ball Buster gives her a dead face.

"I only look Mexican when I'm drowning in tequila," I laugh back. "Haven't had any yet tonight."

Nibbler is quiet, watching her friends interrogate, watching me swivel from one persona to another. She herself is half Japanese. Half Norwegian. A true residualized citizen currently touring me through her friends. The woman looks like the singer Sade. But she is American, in ghetto clothing, and in ghetto vernacular commonly heard in the Federal Heights area of northern Denver. The woman can probably manhandle any man like a Hispanic gangster, even though she is petite.

How and when in the hell did I meet her?

The waitress comes with a tray of cheap tequila. Shit! These women want to drown any of my manhood in booze, to eventually confess something. Ball Buster probably planned all this out. There are twelve shots. 12!

GodDAMN it!

They down a couple like water. I am too old for this crap. My body can not process and hold liquor like it used to. I do not even need all this sin to let go. I want to have something left to father a son and daughter.

Nibbles pushes forward a shot with an intimidating stiff voice, "Down it."

Six eyes are on me. Ball Buster. Her submissive. And Sade.

I shoot one. Their eyes deflate back down. And I say, "Fuck it! I ain't going to church tomorrow," downing the next shot in Irish's honor.

"Is that what Islam people go to? They go to church?"

"Only on Fridays," throwing back to the ignorance. "Friday's their Sunday."

"Do you go to church here?" Blondie pushing further.

"Only on certain Sundays," pushing back gentler.

And then I down another shot. And eventually shouting out a "HELL YEAH!" at them as if I accomplished something worthy, for no reason. In the States, people love to "HELL YEAH!" for sipping toxins, cheering a sports team, walking down a sidewalk on a Saturday night, or knitting, or simply sinning while losing many important brain cells, or thereafter, when promising the night before not to attend church but end up going anyway to dispel a generation worth of immortal acts.

HELL YEAH!

Blondie asks what it is like in Kuwait. I tell the three of them to think of the runs after shooting cheap tequila and eating Taco Bell's burritos way past midnight.

"That bad?" Blondie pushes.

"That much of a twilight zone. And that corrupt."

In reality, there are so many different nationalities racing to acquire the Kuwaiti dinar while trying to hold on to their sense of nationalistic identity as expats. That happens with severe heat 8 months of the year and numerous versions of inshallahs and wallahis.

Ball Buster says, "Stop bitching and leave then. Come back here. Nibbles said you were raised here. Isn't that right?"

This bulldyke is going to harass me all night. I sense it. Drinks will only bring out her aggression.

That fucking Haras.

"Why else would most people stay there?" I tell them. "Lots of money. No taxes. Low work ethic, and shitloads of inshallahs."

"What?" the Bull asks.

"It means 'fuck off' in Kuwaiti Arabic."

She thrusts back her stool, getting angsty.

"Take it easy. That's what they say over there as 'inshallah, habibi,' an idiom thrown loosely to mean—damn—I've been scolded by the term so much that I don't even know what it truly represents anymore."

Nibbles says, "Bitch, please," pushing forward another shot.

Where have I heard that before?

Why am I always harassed?

Fucking Haras, 33, Skin, Tims. Ball Buster. Now, Nibbler.

A live band starts playing on the other side of the massive bar. According to Ball Buster, who's buying the tequila rounds, this place was a furniture warehouse store before it was transferred into decadence. The cover band is playing funk and disco from the 70's and 80's. Some rock. My generation type of music. With how these shots are going to numb, I might as well go out and dance my ass off. Thank goodness for America, where one can diminish his sorrows with a legalized poison. And, it is quite affordable unlike Kuwait, where it is illegal and as expensive as a return airline ticket to Dubai. Why do things have to be so complicated? Legalize the damn poison over there, already!

Most of the people near the floor are caught in the same time period. Feathered hair, goatees, single earrings on men, old Levis 501's over shit-kicking boots, bandanas sticking out of back pockets, and the occasional classic Ray Bans bring out a people who most likely can not address the new rise of Millennial skinny jeans, extensive bearded faces and high voices that make it hard—very hard—to know how they bend sexually. These are blue-collar workers. They are overworked, too exhausted, taxed to hell and back. Drinking, dancing, eating buffalo wings, and talking frankly is their church.

"She's a brick howwsss . . ." the band plays. One matronly lady kicks off the dancing in glitzy jeans and a tit-tight T-shirt.

That is tit. Not tat.

Her feathered hair is gusty, thick, bangs hanging everywhere. Think of hairspray back in the day when it was popular. It is that flashy. She slowly squats and coils down like a true brick house. The jeans should give out and tear up all through her crack. But they stay intact.

Alhamdulillah!

This woman can tear down and chew men from limb to limb. She is a misandrist truly worth submitting to.

Where have these people been in my older years?

A group of bachelorettes comes out on the floor. Bridesmaids and the soon to be bride are all wasted. All of them are wearing party hens on their heads, sets of miniature cocks and balls sprucing up the other floral designs. Two of the maids begin twerking their assess at everyone. The asses are what they like to call stateside, "voluptuous." Or, "curvy."

In Kuwait, they would be considered wide-angled. And, obese.

Here, "voluptuous" and "curvy" are the standard Mac trucks, even though Colorado is one of the fittest and most educated states. Another two bridesmaids are shooting photos of the twerkers. I am guessing the pics will be going off to SnapChat and Instagram for their final filtering before posting as queens of Denver. All of the bachelorettes have come from a table with several huge cocks and balls inflatables that are used as table markers.

How would anyone get lost with Kuwait Towers limping high above? No one surely does back in Kuwait.

I congratulate the bridesmaid by yelling a HELL YEAH in her direction. She signals to join her circle of maids in dancing, shooting some confetti at my face and throwing a cocks and balls rubber trophy into my hands. Then she tilts forward and pecks me on the lips.

How do women do it here? Why in the hell marry if you have any remnants of batshit twerk? Is the men's bachelor party throwing darts around, drinking flat beer and nibbling on peanuts at a retirement home? I sure hope not!

I have a chance to dance alone. The band is funking it out to Prince and Earth Wind and Fire. There is something about letting go to music like letting go to a woman. I can become someone I want to be for that moment. Not the past. Not any future. I become the now. Personalized. Throughout the funky mantras, meditation takes over, putting me into a heightened spell. My heart bleeds out. My soul lives through.

A woman in a cowboy hat comes by and draws close, "Why are you dancing alone? Don't you have a woman?"

"That is my woman," pointing to the band. "It's my frequency."

Her face looks confused. She bends close to my ear again and says, "Are you gay?"

I just look at her and say, "If I am, thank you dearly."

That type of judgment is a huge compliment. Gay men are often very attractive, highly intelligent and groom very well.

Would that judgment be one connotation of a misandrist?

I respond to her stereotype with a juicy smile, "Music is my mistress. I'm dancing with her tonight."

I take a water break in the back of the bar.

Where am I?

Who am I?

Why am I?

Many men on the dance floor are holding drinks in their hands like they are triggering a gun, balancing lack of confidence, triggering a deeper negative spirit to steal, to dispirit sobriety for the night through pleasure. Women have no drinks in hand at all. Their tight jeans, deep valley shirts, and slightly veiled, made up faces sensualize men into submission. It is cunning. Have men get drunk, buy them drinks, and then subvert their patriarchal power into a woman's intricate but confusing inner realm.

Watching people from a near distance helps to understand myself better. All these people are drifting and sifting through one another. They are touring and adjusting into the personalities they deem fit for a special and limited time. They are tourists residing in places and circumstances that make them who and what they are only for that very moment.

Nibbler comes along. She quietly reaches from behind, clenches my groins and nibbles on my earlobe. Her Sade sensuality comes out, in a touch of soft but lightly aggressive street sultriness. The cock grab feels like a clutch with a street weapon. I do not move a smidgen. Then she audaciously pushes away and goes to do the same with one of her lady friends.

Did I just get thugged? Yeah—just got thugged. Inshallah thugged. American style.

I go back out to a corner on the dance floor. Ball Buster shows up and starts shoulder bumping me like a dude to Bad to the Bone song. I can not feel much, though.

That Mexican truth serum.

I am not sure if Ball Buster wants to challenge me to something or is just dancing. I whisper in the Ball Buster's ear, "You love busting my chops, don't you?"

He does not respond.

Yes, he.

The music is so loud. The alcohol louder. Perfect. So, I continue and whisper, "You suur, r a FU-CKA."

Ball Busting Chops laughs back.

Yes, I am drunk.

So is he.

No one gives a rat's ass here. I love it.

Nibbles eventually comes back and asks to take a smoke break outside.

I do not smoke, I tell her. "It's freezing outside."

Colorado temperatures in the middle of winter, and in the middle of the night, can be freezing to death. No gloves, coats, or damn yoga pants will ward off this kind of ice cold for long.

"You will when I show you what I have," nibbling on my neck and singing Sade's the Sweetest Taboo. "Take me to your car."

When we get there, she says, "Really, you drive a mini-van?"

"Best way to be inconspicuous. Got a stick family and an army veteran sticker on the back. Cops think twice."

"Inshallah, habibi," humoring my Kuwaiti into further frustration.

"Who taught you that? I sure didn't! Did you date someone from the Middle East before?"

"You told us earlier." She just keeps on laughing and saying, "Habibi. Omri. Ghalbi. Hayati," all usual Arabic terms of male to female endearment until she says, "Wahashtani el eini," which is a major turn off because the dialect comes out more Egyptian than Kuwaiti.

"Been using Google Translator much?" I ask her.

"Yeah."

"It shows."

"You have kids?" she switches.

"Who doesn't at our age? Don't you have 5?"

"Seven. And, I was just askin'. I was just sayin'."

Inside, Nibbles rolls out a fatty and lights up, not giving a camel's ass what I tell her about not smoking in the car. I examine the almond shaped eyes, dense eyeliner and mascara enclosing greenish eyes, strong cheekbones, and pulsating lips on this woman, and tell her she looks residual. That she could fit in any culture. I also spill that she looks like a woman trapped by time, more by circumstance.

With that description, she reveals how her grandparents and father, as Japanese Americans, were put in a Colorado concentration camp during World War II, because the government had little faith in the making of its new American. She says that many Japanese descendants were even kicked out of western states like California, Arizona, Oregon, and Washington.

Her father met her Scandinavian mother in Denver when she waitressed at a local diner. Love transcended their nationalities into another. Other. Their love transcended into an identity based on mutual respect, honor, decency, to now produce a gorgeous daughter. A gorgeous residue hybrid fitting a generation of smoking legalized marijuana in the Mile High City. What a pot!

Mile High. Where have I heard that before?

Just askin'. Just sayin'.

I harass her left thigh. She looks into the back and asks what the two sleeping bags are for.

Camping, I tell her. "Sometimes I crash back there to get away from too much house comfort, too. Some of my best writing comes out from those bags. Why do you ask?"

"Will ya write me into one of your chapters?"

"Depends on your firework gusto."

"Love when you use vocabulary."

"Is that all it takes?" I toss back. "Simple vocabulary does it to you, huh? Certain words moisten you, do they?"

Damn River Thames and the Brits with their tag questions.

"Dispense the right ones and you shall see."

She gives the Sade look, squeezes my thigh-grabbing hand firmer, puffs out smoke circles into my question, and says, "Just sayin'," with a creamy-looking high and singing "You give me, you give me the sweetest taboo," blowing more smoke into my face, "You give me, you're giving me the sweetest taboo."

Twenty-one.

The front door of the Budweiser Biergarten has a large sign with OPEN on it. Even the business hours state it closes at 9 pm. Why in the hell is it locked? People are roaming around inside. Lights are on.

Come on!

"It can't be closed," a young woman's voice behind me says. I turn around to see her, and she looks like a grad student, probably here to meet more of her college buddies. "Are you part of the Meetup group as well?" she asks.

I turn back and try to jam open the door some more. No use. "Yeah, I'm part of the Meetup." I am sure the group is a singles 30's and 40's. What the hell is she doing here? "Let's go around the back," I tell her.

Walking and bending along the side path and passing a large tent, the young woman is walking in the left corner ahead of me. Why? Am I contagious? She keeps turning back to speak some words, but all I see is ass. It is no ordinary ass. It is slightly curved. The rest of her body is thin, quite thin.

We end up in the back. It is cold outside. Frigid like a bitch. The entire back garden is lit up with Christmas decorations. There is a large inflatable figure that looks like cock and balls.

A Kuwait Towers in a biergarten.

The group is inside. Most of the men are self-preserved in their own space, not talking to the few ladies.

Is this not a singles group?

We introduce ourselves to some of the members and I finally get to know her name. A guy with an elongated face and dark specs tells us we can get free samples out in the tent. Tokens can also be bought for better beers.

Tokens!

Names!

21 and I—yeah, that is what I am going to call her—reach back out bending our way past the cock and balls to get our samples. My Kuwaiti civil ID is checked and she tells the doorwoman that she is with me. No ID is checked. The bar is out of the one and only microbrew. We wait at the table nearby until they restock their beer.

She starts talking about her ex, how he could not produce children, was dispassionate towards her, and how she wanted to live and revel in the moment.

She is a touristy residual, without perhaps knowing it.

Divorce and other painful stories later, we get our first free beer before one of the men from the group inside interrupts us. He clearly wants 21.

We invite him to sit, and he starts unraveling. More stories of detachment, loneliness, and some sexual fantasies stem out.

21 is between 2 older men in their 40's, while she looks

21. 31 is her actual age. Either way, it is trouble. Not *my* sort anyhow.

The two are at it, confessing and addressing until I head inside to the toilet. She joins, leaves him behind. We come back. Deeper experiences flow out. All of us are wires coming out of a bigger mess that took much energy to get out of. Now we are intersecting for a momentary pleasure of humanization.

The guy suddenly appears serious and goes home. I convince 21 to come out with me to an 80's dance night with another Meetup group. A little hesitation later, she agrees. In the minivan, I tell her to see me as her older brother, and I would introduce her to other people her age there.

3 shots in the van, a brisk walk across the street, and we are at Hodi's. I pay her cover, and she goes directly to the bar and asks for a mystery shot. The barman concocts a pink chick drink. She drowns it.

The other 40's group is dancing. 21 is introduced. We dance a song or two. Her eyes change energy to a tantalizing state.

"You're free to roam and meet who ever you like," she says. "You don't need to be with me."

The eyes keep their fix, calling and teasing. Song after song, heat after shadowed heat, our bodies draw closer. Heavier. Deeper.

Her ass starts slightly rubbing on my 4-decade cock, fucking with my hard earned wisdom. She is twisting and gnawing at my torso in a Rocky Mountain version of belly dancing. A few women in a tight group next to us keep staring.

GodDAMN it, 21!

They are the same ones I saw last summer, never knowing if they are gay or straight. When I dance alone, I do not see them looking. When I am with a woman—a very damn young, good-looking woman—stares start flashing. Why does it seem they want to corrupt what is established but not mess with the unestablished?

A man is seen as a creeper when he chooses to dance alone. But he is a keeper when he is out with a younger woman. The keeper is then chewed and spat out during a "relationship" or "commitment," until he once again becomes a creeper.

Women!

A tall semi-blind man is prodding his stick all across the dance floor. He is wearing thick prescription glasses. A woman pities and dances with him.

How long has that scam worked?

I push 21 to the wall off the stage and start ass grabbing, nibbling and mapping her neck. She does something similar, but she pushes away whenever each song heightens to make my semi-hard but wet, divorced self lose control.

I despise losing control. I hate doing it because of a woman, but this young thing is killing it. And she knows and loves it.

I know and love it.

One couple is staring at 21's illustrious by tacit moves of womanhandling a man into loving the hypnosis he goes through.

She is going to terrorize everything I built for myself into submission.

Yes, terrorize. The true and only acceptable term of the word. To-error-ize someone out of his intention into disbelief.

At least that is what she believes.

It is called tantric sex with touches and finesses of wisdom. Five times tonight. I used my 20's and 30's, and

40's, to deliver five long and multipositioned episodes to thwart her youth. To stop her antics in their tracks and turn the entire earlier cockplay into intelligence. Sexual intelligence.

———

New Year's eve is midweek this year. Driving down to Denver is not worth it. 21 comes over. She loves to Lyft ride because she sometimes gets anxious driving. She steps into the kitchen. Shots are taken, music is danced to, hugs are delivered.

We head to the Island Grill. It is packed. Most of the dancers are in their 50's and 60's. Their energy is commendable. They dance in couples. They are older souls who still seek to validate their dying lives through fun.

I will be there soon. I can learn a lot from them.

I introduce her to more resident souls again, but some of these older women are turned off. They hate younger competition. Shit! They hate any female competition.

Dating women my age is hard. They look older than I do. And older women want to rent my body out. Younger ones want to take it for a ride. I do not know who I belong with anymore.

I am fucked either way.

"I love your boots," a young hippie woman says to 21 when we are taking a break at the bar.

"What the hell was that about?" I ask her after she leaves.

"Girl code. She probably assumed I was in trouble. You *do* make me uncomfortable. It probably showed on my face when she came over."

"I do?"

"I can't figure you out," stealing and sipping my beer.

"You're so many people, so many characters at different times."

"Me?" taking back my beer. "Never!"

We dance a little more. An older creeper tries to near 21. I pull her away. The hippie chick draws in from the other corner. I pull 21 near the door. She motions to go minutes before midnight. We head home to usher in a new year, a new touring residency.

I pick her up from her home the next night. Her legs are soft to the eye. She is wearing a tight orange mini dress. Oh, she is going to bring out all sorts of trouble tonight from every direction.

Her dad keeps pestering her to get my number. He is an AB negative, the rarest blood type on Earth. Up to one percent to be exact. I tell her she is protected from both ends, mine and her dad's. Of course, she does not know her own type.

Thanks to America.

The drive down on I-25 is quick. Detailed stories of whim and fancy take over. Our laughs are also the fuel. When we drive into Westminster city limits, I tell her to look at the city building with the Freemason obelisk and the brightly lit apex of the glass triangle on top. How possessed O negatives use it to send messages between themselves and create a hidden history to the rest of the world. How there could be tunnels underneath using fast trains to connect to the rest of their hubs.

Then without notice, the car battery completely dies. Two cop cars show up behind us flashing their lights. It was too fast. How did they show up in seconds?

They are not bullying us, though. Actually, their voices drop to a friendly mode once I talk with them. I ask if they have jumper cables. They tell me they do not have any, and even if they did, they can not jump the car because it goes against regulations. Safety is number one. My van can not be left on the road in the middle of traffic.

That damn obelisk. I talked about them blood types too much. There is no way in hell it was a coincidence that my car shut off like that right in front of that Freemason building.

Signs can reveal so much hidden truth.

They call in a third car to bumper push it to the nearest Walmart. There I can get a new battery. But the car can not even roll into neutral.

Odd.

Even they think it is strange.

Another car comes with a portable jumper. The car is started and the slightly overweight cop says, "HAUL ASS."

"Haul ass, sir?"

"When you take the corner, HAUL ASS."

21 dies laughing, pulls up her mini dress a little to test my control. Her mini dress still keeping me cocked and ready.

BITCH! The good type of bitch. The type that has earned her the confidence and suaveness to thwart most men. Think of ASSHOLE when a guy says it. Similar.

At the next light, it is red. I want to turn, but I can not. The battery dies again. From nowhere and in mere seconds, another cop car drives past us and blocks the back of the van so we do not get into any accident.

This time, a young man with ginger hair comes up with a smug face, throwing around sarcasm. He waits for another cop car. It brings another portable charger. They leave it pressured under my hood while they block off oncoming traffic so I can pull into the Walmart parking lot.

I feel like a dignitary. This should not happen in the States.

Detours.

Inside Walmart, 21 and I feel high. Surreal. We are transiting through aisles of goods, transfusing thoughts to emotions. Emotions to thoughts. It is as if all this detouring is testing our accustomed residencies. It is as if all this surreal detouring is testing our lunacies.

We find the battery, throw it into a cart, pick up an adjustable wrench, and head out to the van.

We must look like two souls who have been lost and found by each other.

Speeding over parking curbs, I launch in the battery, ask her to drive and pick me up near the entrance while I take the old battery to recycle and get my $12 back. Inside, customer service just closed. I push the damn cart outside again and see my van driving to and parking at the outer reaches of the parking lot with no lights. I sweat a little and reach her.

She says it has been a while since she has driven. Lyft's things around. High heels apparently do not help with driving finesse.

We head to a local club. We recollect ourselves in the van by pulling out a few shots and gulps of Apricot Blonde beer. Some kisses and nibbles take hold and create a close space I have forgotten.

It is like the bed space I demand of any person. I can not sleep next to a woman who usually takes nine tenths of my own bed to cuddle me to the edge.

DAMN IT!

Without sleep, everything goes to shit. Let me have my space. This 21 though keeps defying protocol. She just does not care what I say about spatial integrity. Defying it, and me, turns her on.

I must admit, it draws me in.

Walking is therapeutic. I walk near the canal in the neighborhood. Walk along the foothills of the Rockies. I walk in Old Town of Fort Collins trying to absorb how people have made the inanimate historical. It is people who create history. Listening to their stories is a serene walk in itself. Absorbing their energies in different forms is always writing material. It ultimately teaches much more about myself.

The Burmese shop in Old Town has been around for decades. It is loaded with incense and garments adopted from another realm, brought into the Rockies for a connection, converging cultures into a middle point. That point is where definition and identity remain obscure and elusive to so many. It is residual. Touristy residual.

The Burmese woman asks if I am Burmese.

I ask why and tell her no.

"You sure look Burmese," she says.

"Thank you."

I engage her to listen to her soul. People rarely do that nowadays amongst capitalism. I am not sure why people like to reveal themselves in front of me. Stories that seem to be hidden amongst their loved ones come alive to a stranger like a residual tourist. Is it because I am a stranger? Or because I have a shifty aura, like a temporary Burmese, that makes them want to confess mosaics of themselves?

She begins to complain about the Burmese police and other authorities who expect bakhsheesh—tips—just to bring legal things into the country.

"When I went there after the major earthquake, a police officer wouldn't let me pass customs until I paid him off."

"What did you take?"

"A few books and clothing for the needy. The cop wanted a tip for importing donations."

Sounds like the Middle East. Nothing is ever clear. Sounds like many developing countries.

While aimlessly walking in Old Town Square, I stumble upon Indigo Rose Bookstore, nestled between a tattoo parlor and bar. I walk upstairs and inside, and lo and behold, the place is a treasure trove of books—comfortably messily stacked books. They smell musky and sweet: chocolaty and coffeeyee. Sights and smells that awaken urges to wonder and wander through other people's words. That is how bookstores used to be. How they should be.

The owner stands up from a comfortably beaten leather reading chair and starts giving a personal tour. Gray hair, hardened skin, and a slouched back can not hold back the geyser of energy this man has. He explains how the hardwood floors in one room are the 1800's originals. Explains how he is not in the book business for money. I witness how he cares so much for the written word that they translate to human intersections for him.

The intersections. The wires. The tourism.

Then he gleefully dishes out stories of Hemingway, train rides on the Patagonia, and winds down to reveal stories of his personal friends who exited this world, while insulated by thousands of other people's words in novels, anthologies, books of poetry, and philosophies, amongst 1890's brick walls that have accrued historical stories of their own. The proprietor does not watch TV, never advertises his bookstore, relies on word of mouth, despises technology, and is especially uncomfortable with today's cell phone addiction—of people who seek to draw close but end up more isolated.

We discuss support for local authors, and without hesitation he welcomes selling my last book. Without any consignment.

I purchase one Hemingway and a Faulkner. He tallies the price including tax on a notepad. Technology is left forward for the masses who have been conditioned to depend on it.

The experience is better than going to a coffee shop. His modest wisdom and compassion brings out a rare smile in me. Brings out a fancy to write about this because it is worth remembering, like a photo that can stimulate numerous perceptions; countless descriptions.

The man is a walking library of information. People should support their local artists in whatever form they display their creativity. They just require a little attentive time. That short but dense attention comes back as a book form. Musings and varied knowledge are surely better than submitting one's soul to a digital, virtual cloud.

Walking farther down Linden Street, I cross Jefferson and see some new establishments sprucing up the River District, slowly Lego-building the new and extravagant for the haves and hipsters to throw temporary money into. The have-nots are across the street sitting and standing, corrupted and detached from the hoopla.

Christians on one side are living lavishly for a borrowed time while on the other side Christians are trying to save and reinsert the homeless as productive citizens in their version of the same society.

It is a wonderful mess.

It is the homeless shelter that stands out. What a sore eye to many. This Christian homeless shelter is backed by the Denver one in the LoDo district.

One man is slouching on a bench with his legs spread out, throwing coach-like pointy fingers at large vehicles. He is wearing many uneven layers of clothing to fight off the winter cold. Clothes he has probably found and that have been donated to him. They are all out of fashion; they are all out of sync.

A brittle beard, drab hair, thick skin, and a hoarse voice give this man—this being—distinction. I am not talking distinction among the other homeless people, but among the homed. He is murmuring things to himself, escalating phrases to only drop them to low octaves. Sounds and utterances other homeless people could decode but not when it comes to a supposed civilized being like me. It is also a scare tactic to ward off people like the haves across the street who are drinking merrily and have been celebrating the holidays, gluttonously.

There is a large dark green backpack to his side. Ripped plastic bags surround him. A slightly defeated aluminum container is between his legs.

One piece of garment stands out the most amongst his layers. Just one. The green army jacket is buried in the middle, a fatigue which has most likely fatigued his innocent soul for killing peoples in foreign lands that he had no intention in provoking. I can not give this man a nickname like I often do to individuals who catch and get caught up by a specific time in which they shine as heroes. This person is a lost hero.

What is he waiting for? Most would rather end life than struggle through this. Why is this man holding on? I am sure many haves try to come up and save him.

I sit next to him on the bench. I do not greet him as a have would. I just sit as if I need to, as if I have to. I do not want to save him. Hell, he does not even look like he wants to be saved. He wants to stay drowning.

Minutes that feel like hours pass by. Neither of us is saying anything. His voice scare tactics have stopped. Sure, he gives some glances. I can feel his eyes scratching at my body. But they are warming my soul instead. He should be apprehensive. The man has probably seen much more in one year than a lifetime a have has ever seen.

I do not know what I am doing, but it feels comfortable to give up on this reality of success, of a hollowed out soul. A man, who has been warred, financially succeeded, fruitfully yet temporarily fathered, suddenly divorced, and left out to whither as a homeless spirit amongst debauchery in the midst of other souls, makes me as much of haved have-not as the man next to me.

I quickly turn around to the sound of an empty bottle hitting the pavement, but it does not break. There is an echoing, vibrating, lingering low pitch to the sound. The homeless guy twitches spastically a little. Above the fallen bottle on the wall is a slightly ripped poster reading:

PTSD?
NOT ONLY WAR VETERANS GET IT.
CIVILLIANS TOO!

ABOUT THE AUTHOR

Haitham Alsarraf is the author of *Glass Seeds, Inshallah, Habibi* and *Invasion Occupation Awakening*. He has founded and edited two literary magazines, *Kaleidoscope* and *Perceptions*. Haitham's works have been published in numerous literary magazines across the globe such as *Failbetter*. His books have made the top #12 bestselling category in the United Kingdom and top #41 in the United States on Amazon. He currently teaches English at Kuwait University.